WE WERE THERE
AT
PEARL HARBOR

"Jeff! It's the Japs! They've done it!"

WE WERE THERE
AT
PEARL HARBOR

By FELIX SUTTON

Historical Consultant:
VICE ADMIRAL WILLARD A. KITTS, 3rd
USN (Retired)

Illustrated by FRANK VAUGHN

Publishers
GROSSET & DUNLAP
NEW YORK

PRINTED IN THE UNITED STATES OF AMERICA
LIBRARY OF CONGRESS CATALOG CARD NO. 57-10106

We Were There at Pearl Harbor

For
MIKE

Contents

Illustrations

WE WERE THERE
AT
PEARL HARBOR

CHAPTER ONE

A Quiet Sunday Morning

THE day started out like all days in Hawaii. If anything, the sky was brighter and bluer than usual on this quiet Sunday morning. And the sun was big and round and red as it climbed up over the crest of Diamond Head and spilled its pale gold shafts of light down the steep mountain slope and into the open window of Mike Morrison's bedroom.

Mike opened an eye, yawned, and stretched his arms lazily over his head.

The early morning air was sweet and cool, and heavy with the spicy perfume of hibiscus and oleander. In the trees on the lawn outside, Mike could hear the raucous yak-yak-yaking of the myna birds as they argued and quarreled with each other. From far away, somewhere down in Pearl Harbor, came the deep-toned whistle of a tugboat going about its morning chores.

Mike stretched again and wondered whether he ought to get up or roll over and catch another forty winks. After all, it was Sunday and no school to worry about . . .

Holy Cow! Sunday—December 7th—his birthday!

Mike leaped from the bed like a spring that has suddenly become uncoiled. He climbed into polo shirt, shorts, and sneakers, raced to the bathroom where he gave his teeth a quick swipe with a toothbrush, splashed cold water on his face, ran a wet comb once-over-lightly through his hair, and then pounded down the stairs to the dining room.

His father was already at the table eating breakfast, the four broad stripes of a captain of the Regular Navy gleaming on the shoulder boards of his white uniform.

"Well, good morning," Captain Morrison said, smiling. "I was afraid you weren't going to get up in time for me to wish you a happy birthday before I shoved off."

He pushed his chair back from the table, got

[4]

to his feet, threw Mike a smart regulation Navy salute, and stuck out a big hand.

"Happy birthday, son! How does it feel to be fourteen years old?"

Mike grinned. Before he could think of a good answer, Lieutenant Jeff Morrison breezed into the room. Instead of the full uniform of an Army Air Corps pilot that he usually wore, this morning he was dressed in an old khaki Army shirt and faded trousers, and wore a much-scuffed pair of canvas sneakers on his feet.

He aimed a left jab at Mike's chin, and when the boy ducked, clamped a headlock on him and began to give the top of his red head a vigorous Dutch rub with the knuckles of his right hand. As Mike wriggled out of the hold, Jeff slapped him on the shoulder and stepped back laughing.

"So the kid brother is fourteen! Let me look at you."

He looked Mike up and down, like a painter trying to decide whether a picture is good or bad, and then gravely nodded his head.

"Yes," he said. "You do seem a little taller than you did yesterday. It won't be long before we'll be ready to measure you for an Air Corps uniform."

"Air Corps, my foot!" Captain Morrison snorted. "I hope I've raised at least one intelligent son. When this boy grows into a uniform, it's going to be Navy blue."

Jeff winked at his father. "Well, I'm willing to concede one thing," he said. "Today he's going to be more interested in boats than airplanes."

A big smile lighted up the captain's face. "And I'm willing to concede that for once the Army is right. Today, Mike will be strictly Navy."

Puzzled, Mike looked from his father to his big brother.

"Say, what is this?" he wanted to know.

"Well, I'll tell you," Jeff said. "Yesterday I was walking down past the Yacht Club dock, and out there tied up to a buoy was the slickest little sailboat I ever saw. She was brand, spanking new. Her hull was painted oyster-white, and the name on her stern was *Mister Mike*. I asked a fellow who owned her, and he said that some Navy captain had bought her for his kid as a birthday present. Some guy named Norrison or Forrison or—"

Mike's eyes grew saucer-wide, and his mouth popped open.

"Gosh, Dad!" he finally managed. "Gosh, Dad, do you really mean—"

Captain Morrison patted him affectionately on the arm.

"Well, now," he said, "every fourteen-year-old sailor's son ought to have his own boat. Have fun with her, Mike." Then he added, "By golly, if I didn't have a staff meeting this morning, I'd go out with you on her maiden voyage."

"Well, I don't have any staff meeting," Jeff said. "How about the Air Corps crewing for you, skipper?"

Mike grabbed his brother by the arm.

"Gee, Dad," he said, "thanks a million! Come on, Army. What are we waiting for?"

As he spoke, his mother entered from the kitchen carrying a steaming platter of bacon and eggs.

"For one thing," she announced, "you boys are going to wait until you've had some breakfast."

She put the platter down on the table and stood on tiptoe to kiss her tall young son lightly on the cheek.

"Happy birthday, little boy," she said.

The radio on the sideboard had been playing a soft, haunting Hawaiian tune, "The Song of the Islands." Suddenly the music stopped and an announcer's voice broke in:

"This is a special news announcement. The

[7]

Japanese ambassador to Washington, Admiral Nomura, and the Special Envoy, Mr. Kurusu, yesterday held an hour-long conference with Secretary of State Cordell Hull. Unofficial reports indicate that a peaceful solution to the differences between

the governments of Japan and the United States may yet be reached. The President has made a personal appeal to Emperor Hirohito to withdraw Japanese troops from Indo-China, and the feeling in Washington news circles is that . . ."

[8]

Mrs. Morrison snapped off the set.

"War!" she said. "I wish they'd stop talking about war!"

Mike looked up from his scrambled eggs.

"How about it, Dad?" he asked. "Is the Navy worried much about this talk of a Jap invasion?"

Captain Morrison looked thoughtful.

"No . . . not too seriously worried," he said. "There's no question but what the Japs are up to something. These peace talks in Washington are very likely a stall. But Staff doesn't think they'll try to hit us here. If and when they decide to start something, the logical direction for them to move would be against the East Indies."

"But just the same," Jeff put in, "they could give the Navy a rough going-over if they attacked Pearl Harbor without warning. Your big battlewagons are lined up alongside Ford Island like ducks in a shooting gallery."

"Yes," the captain admitted, "they probably could. But there's not much chance that they'd try. You see, in order to throw an attacking force at Pearl, they'd have to divide their Combined Fleet. And whether you like the Japs or not, you've got to admit the little devils are too smart to do a fool thing like that."

[9]

"Let's just pray they don't attack anywhere at all," Mrs. Morrison said fervently.

"Don't worry, Mother," Captain Morrison assured her. "Our carriers are out on maneuvers, and our subs maintain a tight patrol at all times. So I don't think there's much danger to the islands. Not on such a lovely morning as this."

Mike forked the last bite of egg into his mouth and jumped up from his chair.

"This lovely morning is going to be half gone before I get down to my boat. How about it, Air Corps? Let's scramble!"

"Right with you, skipper!" Jeff replied, and the two brothers raced out the door.

As Mike rounded a turn in the walk to get to Jeff's convertible in the garage, a familiar voice spoke softly from the other side of the hibiscus hedge that separated the Morrisons' lawn from that of their next-door neighbors.

"Morning, Mike."

Mike groaned. "Oh, no! Not you again!"

It was Mary Jane Fisher, the daughter of Captain Morrison's executive officer. Mary Jane was a year younger than Mike. Her jet-black hair was cut in a long bob, and she wore a crisp, red cotton dress.

"I hear you got a new boat for your birthday," she said. "May I go with you to try her out?" She hesitated. "Please, Mike!"

Mike sniffed. "Boats are no place for a girl. Why don't you stay home and play with your dolls?"

Mary Jane's voice sounded hurt. "All right, Mike." She held out something in her hand. "This is for you."

It was a beautiful waterproof wrist watch, real

Air Corps style, with a sweep second hand and a stop timer.

"Gosh!" Mike said.

Jeff laughed. "Now doesn't that make you feel kind of mean, skipper? Don't you think that rates a ride on the *Mister Mike?*"

The chrome of the new watch gleamed in the sun as Mike slipped it on his wrist.

"Gosh, Mary Jane!" he said again. "This sure is nice. Why, sure—sure. Hop in and let's go."

Jeff parked the car at the Yacht Club dock, and the tender took them out to the *Mister Mike*. She was a beautiful little boat, that was certain. Mike's hands shook with excitement as he broke out her spotless white sails and ran them up the slender mast. Then Mike took the tiller, Jeff cast off from the mooring, and the trim little craft caught a spanking breeze that blew down off the top of the Koolau Range, and danced merrily over the sun-lit water into East Loch.

They sailed north up the Loch, Mike getting the feel of his new boat and heeling her close into the wind for the sheer joy of watching her keen prow cut a foamy path through the clear, blue water.

Then he tacked and came smartly down between the rows of destroyers and supply ships that were anchored side by side in that part of the harbor. Lolling back in the cockpit, he could see the Navy crews bustling about on the decks, polishing brass and going through their routine morning duties.

Almost bursting with pride, Mike gave the order: "Come about!"

Jeff released the sheets, the boom slapped sharply across the deck, the sail caught the wind from its new quarter, and the *Mister Mike* scudded down the narrow channel between Ford Island and the Naval Station.

Now they were sailing down Pearl Harbor's famous Battleship Row. Here were the powerful and deadly battlewagons that were the pride of the United States Navy, America's first line of defense. The *Nevada,* the *West Virginia,* the *Oklahoma,* the *Arizona,* the *Tennessee,* the *Maryland,* the *California* . . . all lined up in orderly precision, beam to beam and bow to stern, riding gently at their moorings and seeming to slumber in the morning sun.

On the deck of the *Nevada,* as they passed, the ship's band was forming up to play morning colors. The crisp commands of the officers came over the water with startling clearness.

Mike leaned back and cradled the tiller in the

crook of his right arm. The bright Hawaiian sun shone full into his face. A spindrift of fleecy clouds floated slowly, high overhead. Jeff and Mary Jane lay sprawled on the deck, soaking up the sun.

Mike glanced at his new watch. The hands said 7:55. He translated that into Navy talk—zero seven hundred and fifty-five hours. 7th December, 1941.

Looking lazily upward, Mike saw what seemed to be a tiny, black speck hurtling down out of the blue sky. In seconds, it took on the shape of a low-winged airplane. It was followed by another, then

a third, and then by a whole formation of twenty
or more. The planes barreled downward in a steep
dive.

"Hey, Jeff," he called carelessly. "Looks like the
Air Corps is out having fun this morning."

Jeff shaded his eyes with his hand.

"Those guys must be crazy," he said, sitting up

suddenly. "They'll get the book thrown at them for buzzing the harbor like this. They're nuts!"

At that instant, a small, dark object detached itself from the underside of the lead plane and tumbled earthward, making a shrill, whistling scream as it came. It hit the afterdeck of the *Arizona,* and a great black cloud of oily smoke mushroomed up out of the flame of the ear-splitting explosion. The big battlewagon reeled under the force of the blow.

The plane zoomed up to regain altitude and Mike could see the red ball of the Rising Sun painted on the tips of its wings.

Jeff jumped to his feet. His mouth was open, his eyes wide and staring in disbelief.

"This is no kidding!" he yelled. "This is it!"

Mike gripped the tiller with hands that were shaking and suddenly wet with sweat.

"Jeff! It's the Japs! They've done it!"

CHAPTER TWO

Fiery Inferno

IN THE next few terrifying seconds, the whole harbor exploded before Mike's disbelieving eyes in one great, deafening, fiery upheaval.

Jap planes screamed down out of nowhere, coming in from every angle at once. A moment ago the sky had been clear, and empty of everything but a few fleecy clouds. Now it was suddenly black with vicious killers, ruthlessly dropping their torpedoes and bombs on the defenseless ships and spraying streams of bullets from their machine guns like jets of liquid fire from a hose.

The dull, thudding *br-oom, br-oom, br-oom, br-oom* of the bomb blasts followed each other in such continuous succession that they finally blended and merged together in Mike's ears as one giant, echoing roar. Columns of fire and smoke leaped up from a dozen targets at once, and the greasy smoke pillars flowed together and formed a huge, black suffocating cloud over the harbor, blotting out the sun.

From every ship anchored on Battleship Row came the deep, growling squawk of the klaxon horns as they frantically sounded General Quarters.

Beyond the line of battleships, the shore installations on Ford Island began to go up in volcanic eruptions of smoke and flames.

Out in the harbor, a destroyer—or a tender, Mike couldn't be sure just what it was—took a direct hit down her funnel and exploded in a blinding flash of light.

As Jeff had remarked at breakfast, the big battleships were "sitting ducks." They lay so close together that any bomb that missed one target was almost sure to hit another.

A Jap bored in for the stern of the *Nevada* and released his bomb. He was too high. The bomb lobbed down in a slow arc like a tennis ball—over the *Nevada*, over the *Arizona*, and exploded against the side of the *West Virginia* with a great, resounding *wh-o-om!*

The *California* caught a torpedo that had been intended for the ship berthed next to her. She shuddered and rolled, and almost put her beam under the water. Then she righted herself, like a canoe passing through the wake of a speeding motorboat, and almost immediately took another "fish" in her side. This time, almost as though she were too tired, she didn't roll with the blow, but a great column of fire roared up from her afterdeck.

A Navy "honey barge" that had been leisurely collecting garbage from the fleet when the attack began, took a hit from a low-level bomber. She came apart at the seams and sank like a rock. The garbage she had been carryi   d out over the water. A head of cabbage,   ong by the swell, bumped against the hull of   *Mister Mike*.

Mike couldn't believe it. For months there had been talk of war. And now this was it! No warning! Just a death-rain of bombs on a peaceful Sunday morning!

A bomb that had managed to miss all the ships entirely, dropped with a great splash into the water not twenty feet ahead of the little sailboat. By a miracle, it failed to explode, but the waves it kicked up rocked the *Mister Mike,* and the mighty splash of water soaked everyone on board.

Neither Jeff nor Mary Jane had said a word since the bombing started. Or, if they had, Mike had been too stunned to hear them.

Now the *ack-ack-ack* of machine-gun fire became a new sound in the ear-splitting noise of the battle.

Some of the antiaircraft crews on the American ships had recovered from the bewildering shock of the attack, and were beginning to fight back. From the foretop of the *Maryland* a machine gun opened up and added its staccato clatter to the crashing din of the exploding bombs. Guns from most of the other battlewagons and cruisers joined in the pounding chorus.

A Jap plane dove down at the *Arizona's* fantail. Tracers from three machine-gun crews drilled into it, and it crashed into the water, not fifty feet from the *Mister Mike,* exploding into a thousand pieces.

Almost at the same time, torpedoes smashed into the sides of the *Oklahoma,* the *West Virginia,* and the *Arizona,* detonating with loud, hollow booms and sending geysers of water high into the air. Mike saw the body of a man hurled skyward by one of the explosions. It turned over and over as it rose upward, like a lifeless rag doll, and then dropped into the water.

The frail little *Mister Mike* pitched and bucked in the swells like a frightened bronc, as the quiet waters of Pearl Harbor were churned into fury by the explosion of the bombs and the rolling of the stricken ships.

Through the thick clouds of smoke that swirled all around them, Mike could see Jeff clawing at the sails. In desperation, he hacked at the lines with his knife, and the mainsail came fluttering down the mast and collapsed over the boom.

"The motor!" Jeff yelled, screaming over the din. "Start the motor, kid!"

Mike punched the starter button of the little auxiliary engine, and it sputtered into life. Then Jeff was at his side and grabbed the tiller from his hand.

"Now let's see if we can get out of here," he panted.

He put the tiller hard over, and the *Mister Mike* slid under the great curving bow of a battleship that loomed high over them like a towering, gray steel wall.

Out of the corner of his eye, Mike saw Mary Jane crouched down in the cockpit. Her eyes were big and white with terror. Mike managed a feeble smile and tried to act as though he wasn't scared half to death. "I told you boats were no place for a girl," he heard himself saying.

The shriek of a diving plane jerked his eyes upward. As he looked, the Jap released his bomb on the battlewagon they had just passed under and then strafed her decks with his guns. Zooming over the ship, the plane came straight for the sailboat, the machine guns in its nose stabbing out with fingers of fire and the bullets marching in a straight line of vicious splashes over the water.

As they approached the *Mister Mike,* the marching bullets spattered across her glistening deck, kicking up a row of splinters as they went past. The mast cracked and slowly began to topple over. The tiller took a direct hit and was hammered out of Jeff's hands. The little boat stopped dead, as though it had run headlong into a stone jetty, wallowed for a moment in the swell, and then staggered forward again.

Mike turned his head just in time to see the plane take the full fire of a battery of machine guns from a cruiser. It vanished in a ball of flame before it plunged into the water.

"The lines, Mike!" Jeff yelled. "Cut away the lines!"

Mike yanked out his knife and slashed at the

lines that still secured the broken top half of the mast, now trailing over the side. Then he watched the slender stick free itself in the water and slowly drift astern.

Ever since the first bomb had exploded, Mike had been in a daze, almost a state of shock. He knew this awful thing was happening, but his mind stubbornly refused to believe what his ears were hearing and his eyes were seeing. In spite of his brave words to Mary Jane and his prompt obedience of Jeff's orders, he had been moving about like a boy in a nightmare. It had been as though he were completely detached from this terrible inferno that had flamed up, out of nothing, all around him.

But the damage to his own *Mister Mike* suddenly cleared his head and snapped him back to reality. Instinctively, he experienced the same feeling as the captains of all these other fine ships that were taking such a beating.

His ship had been attacked! *His* crew had been shot at! He wanted to fight back!

The blood throbbed in his temples, and he found himself standing up on the deck holding onto the stump of the mast, shaking his fist at the diving Jap planes and yelling.

[23]

Jeff's quiet voice came through the noise of his own shouting and the ceaseless blasting of the exploding bombs.

"Take it easy, skipper! Take it easy!"

Jeff pulled him down into the precarious shelter of the cockpit.

"The first rule of battle, kid," he said, "is to present the smallest possible target to the enemy. Stay alive until you have a chance to fight."

Mike grinned. Funny, he thought, he wasn't half as scared as he had been a minute ago. He glanced at Mary Jane. Her face and her dress were black with smoke, but the first look of terror was

gone from her face. She made a weak effort to smile, and he patted her on the shoulder.

"You're doing all right," he said.

Jeff struggled with the tiller that had been half shot away by the machine-gun fire. The little boat was sluggish but still making headway.

"Hang on!" he said. "We'll try to make the Navy Yard dock."

The *Mister Mike* took a sudden lurch as another explosion, the loudest yet, rocked the harbor. A high wall of fire spouted up from the *Arizona,* and the big battlewagon listed like a prizefighter whose legs have been turned to rubber by a heavy blow on the chin. Slowly—almost like slow motion in the movies, Mike thought—she started to list and go down by the bow.

Mike stared, and expelled his breath in a long, silent whistle.

"Look at that, Jeff! Look at that! They must have hit her powder magazine!"

Another Jap plane flashed overhead, strafing as it came. The line of marching bullets splashed past not ten feet from the sailboat's beam.

By now the smoke-darkened sky was thick with planes, the Japs buzzing in and out of the billowing black clouds like a swarm of angry hornets.

A torpedo plane started its low, swooping run for the side of the already sinking *West Virginia*. A machine gun from the flaming deck of the big ship caught it in a stream of tracers as it came in, hit the torpedo slung underneath its fuselage, and the plane disintegrated in a blazing shower of fire.

Small pieces of it rained down on the deck of the sailboat. Mike felt a bee-sting on his right arm and saw that it was bleeding from a small cut. He looked around quickly. Yes, Jeff and Mary Jane were okay.

"This is getting too close for comfort," Jeff yelled. "Keep your heads down, kids!"

At that moment, Mike's eyes caught a movement in the water. It was a man, threshing his arms feebly and struggling to swim through the film of oil. Mike shook Jeff's arm and pointed.

Jeff put the broken tiller over, and the *Mister Mike* came slowly around. Then he cut the motor, and the sluggish boat slid up to the drowning man.

Mike grasped him by the hands and tried to pull him over the side. His fingers slipped on the greasy coating of oil that covered the man from head to foot, and the sailor, unable to help himself, slid back into the water.

Without hesitating, Mike jumped in after him.

Getting a firm hold on the collar of his shirt, he swam with him to the stern of the boat. Jeff threw a line overboard and Mike secured it under the sailor's armpits. Then he clambered up, and the combined strength of the two brothers dragged the man over the rail.

The sailor was gasping for breath, and his eyes were staring wide with shock and fright. He slumped against the side of the cockpit. His eyes closed and he lay still.

No sooner had Jeff put the little boat back on

her erratic course for the dock than Mike tugged at his arm again. Over there, much farther away this time, was another swimming man.

He was lifting his big arms high out of the water in a powerful crawl, and his kicking feet trailed a wake of foam behind him. Between every stroke, he yelled at the crew of the small boat in a loud, lusty voice.

"Hey!" A stroke. "Hey, you guys!" Another stroke. "Over here!"

When Jeff brought the boat around to him, the sailor grabbed the gunwale and pulled himself on board with a mighty heave. He shook his head, and his white teeth flashed in a grin through the black oil that streaked his face.

"You know," he said in a thick Southern drawl, "you fellows ought to get in to shore. A man could get hurt out here."

CHAPTER THREE

The Navy Fights Back

JEFF gunned the engine of the little boat and leaned into the crippled tiller.

"Friend," he said to the grinning sailor, "that's exactly what we're trying to do. I want to land these kids and then get out to Wheeler Field. If my P-40 is still there, I've got a job to do."

Mike had to shout to make himself heard over the thunder of the bombing.

"You think they've hit the airfields, Jeff?"

"They must have," Jeff shouted back. "I don't see any of our boys up there. But I just hope there's one fighter left for me."

His sentence was drowned out by two violent explosions that came in rapid succession, torpedo hits on the already dying *Oklahoma*. Shrouded in a thick veil of smoke, she slowly began to capsize, like a whale that has been struck by a harpoon and, in its death agonies, rolls over on its back.

"Look at her!" the sailor said, his voice suddenly solemn. "They told us those battlewagons couldn't sink or turn over. But look at her!"

The *Oklahoma* slowly, awkwardly, put her port beam under the water. Men scrambled over her starboard rail and began to climb up on her rounded keel. She kept on rolling until her tall masts finally dug into the muddy bottom of Pearl Harbor. Then with a gigantic, spasmodic shudder, she came to rest.

Her bottom, lying exposed to the smoke-filled air, and with the shafts of her screws jutting out at odd angles, was covered with men like ants swarming over an anthill.

A Jap *Zero* fighter came in low and splattered the crouching men with a vicious burst of bullets from its guns.

The sailor began yelling and shaking his fist at the planes as Mike had done.

"Get me to a gun! Get me to a gun and give me a crack at those dirty little—"

Another ship off to the right went up in a roaring fountain of smoke and fire and cut off the sailor's words. Mike yanked him by the arm and yelled in his ear.

"Come and help me with this other man," he shouted.

As they turned, Mike saw that Mary Jane was already doing all she could for the unconscious

man. She held his head in her lap and was trying to clean the scum of oil from his face with a dirty rag.

The man's head lolled back, his mouth open. He was mumbling, out of his head. Mary Jane tried to comfort him, as a mother soothes a sick child.

Suddenly, up ahead of them, a destroyer opened fire. But instead of shooting into the air, she was firing into the water. The shells from her deck guns smacked into the choppy surface and exploded with hollow, underwater *bl-a-ams!* that sent little geysers of water spouting into the air.

Her crew was working frantically with the depth-charge releases on her stern. Then the "ash-cans" began to roll down the ramp and splash into the water.

Three seconds after the first depth charge disappeared, there was a booming, ear-shattering roar, and the sea blossomed up in a gigantic mushroom of water and white spray.

"How about that?" Jeff yelled in the sailor's ear. "They must have caught a sub!"

"You're crazy!" the sailor yelled back. "There can't be any Jap subs in the harbor."

"There can't be any Jap bombers in the air,

either," Jeff said, raising his voice above the awful din. "But whatever those things are up there, they're doing a lot of damage."

The depth charges from the destroyer continued to churn up the already raging water of Pearl Harbor. Mike's little sailboat reeled and pitched, put her beam ends under and sloshed water over the soaked and shivering occupants of the cockpit.

Then a long, black metal object that looked like the nose of a shark jutted up from the water, ahead of the *Mister Mike*. It hung in the air for a moment, as if gasping for breath, and then slid back under the surface, leaving a little swirling eddy out of which a series of air bubbles gurgled and popped.

The sailor slapped Mike on the back like a rooter at a football game.

"By gosh, you're right!" he screamed in Mike's ear. "That was a sub, sure enough!" He began to laugh, almost hysterically. "Man," he shouted, "this is some fight! I sure wish I had a gun!"

"It may be a good fight," Jeff yelled back, "but we've got no business being in it."

He leaned into the broken tiller and headed the boat toward the Navy Yard dock.

How they got through the jumbled swarm of

crippled, burning, sinking ships Mike never knew.

The mighty *West Virginia* was sinking, her whole port side ripped out of her by a barrage of Jap torpedoes. The *Nevada's* decks were on fire, and the forward part of the ship was a huge pile-up of tangled wreckage. But smoke was coming up from her funnels and she was beginning, slowly and laboriously, to move out of Battleship Row and down the narrow channel under her own power.

The *Oklahoma* was finished. The *Maryland,* pinned between the overturned *Oklahoma* and the dockside, was smoking from a succession of bomb-hits, but all her antiaircraft guns were in action, hammering away at the screeching enemy planes overhead.

The *California* was going down, her decks and superstructure ablaze. The proud *Arizona,* on fire from bow to stern, was rapidly listing and sinking. From the decks of the *Tennessee,* geysers of flame shot upward. She, too, was pinned to the dock by the bulk of the sinking *West Virginia.*

But from every deck that was still above water, the guns of the U. S. Navy were fighting back. The firing was uneven and not always accurate. But every now and then—just often enough to give the men encouragement and send them into wild,

roaring cheers—a Jap plane was stopped in mid-air by a burst of fire and dropped with a blazing flash into the water.

Mike's heart pounded with pride at the sight of these Americans fighting like demons against such overwhelming odds. But it sank in despair at the awful shambles Pearl Harbor had become.

Only half an hour ago, the sprawling harbor had been serene and quiet, lazing under the brilliant morning sun, with the sound of church bells pealing softly over the water and the ships of the world's most powerful navy riding peacefully at their anchor chains.

And now that great fleet was a burning, sinking junkpile.

Mike's eyes burned. He knew it wasn't only the acrid smoke that made the tears run down his cheeks.

He remembered the conversation with his father at the breakfast table. It didn't seem possible that it had been less than an hour ago! It seemed like another time and another world. Anyway, the Big Brass, whoever they were—the guys who sat behind their desks and tried to figure out where the Japs would and wouldn't strike—had sure figured this one wrong.

He had a sudden, sickening thought. Mom and Dad! Had the Japs bombed the houses up on Makalapa? He didn't see how it was possible, but . . .

The bow of the little boat bumped gently against the pilings of the Navy Yard dock.

"Make her fast, Mike," Jeff said, shouting to make himself heard above the undulating roar of the bombardment that was steadily pounding the fleet.

Mike grabbed for a handhold on the ladder, then ducked as a bomb smashed into a warehouse on the dock and sent a shower of splinters and wood fragments cascading all around them.

He tied the painter that trailed from the bow of

the *Mister Mike* to a rung of the ladder and turned around. The sailor with the Southern drawl had thrown the unconscious man over his shoulder. Carrying him as easily as a sack of flour, he went up the ladder and disappeared over the edge of the dock above.

"Up you go, kids," Jeff said, pushing Mike and Mary Jane up the ladder ahead of him. He herded them into the shelter of what remained of the bombed-out warehouse.

"You can't stay here," he declared, when they had stretched the sailor out on the floor and made him as comfortable as possible. "I'll go around by Makalapa on my way to Wheeler and drop you off at home."

"How about it, Jeff?" Mike asked. "Can I go to Wheeler with you?"

"Nothing doing, buster," Jeff said sternly. "You've had enough for one day. After all that out there," he waved his hand in the direction of the flaming, smoking harbor, "you're lucky you got this far. You're lucky you didn't—"

Again the crash of a bomb explosion cut off Jeff's words in mid-sentence. A spout of water geysered into the air two hundred feet from the dock. A small motor launch that had been picking up survivors rode part way up the waterspout and then overturned, spilling men in all directions.

Mike dashed for the ladder.

"You take Mary Jane home," he called over his shoulder. "I'll be okay."

He scrambled down the ladder, untied the painter, and kicked over the engine of the *Mister Mike*.

"Hey! Come back here!" It was Jeff, shouting angrily above the din. "Come back here, you crazy—"

"Relax!" Mike called back. "I've got to get out to those men!"

The Southern sailor started after him.

"Hey, wait for me! You'll need help!"

The motor caught. Mike put the boat sharply about and headed for the men who were milling around in the water, desperately clutching at the remains of the launch.

"Well, of all the . . ." A big grin creased Jeff's face. This kid brother of his was quite a guy! Someday he'd really fill out that Air Corps uniform! *Someday?* Doggone it, he was a first-class fightin' man right now!

Jeff took Mary Jane gently by the arm.

"Let's go, honey," he said. "If I can find a jeep that is still in one piece, it's high time I took you home."

"But how about him?" Mary Jane said, pointing to the sailor who still lay unconscious on the warehouse floor. "We can't leave him like this."

Jeff sighed. "You kids will be the death of me yet. All right. Give me a hand."

With Mary Jane's help, Jeff slung the wounded man over his shoulder in a fireman's-carry and started out the door.

A *Zero,* finishing its run on one of the ships in the harbor, strafed the dock with a burst of machine-gun bullets as they made a dash for the road.

CHAPTER FOUR

On Wheeler Field

JEFF found an abandoned Navy pick-up truck standing in the street behind the warehouse. It was covered with dust and ashes, and a gaping hole had been torn in the roof of the cab. But as far as he could see, it hadn't been seriously damaged by Jap machine-gun slugs or flying metal from the bursting bombs.

He put the sailor into the front seat, and Mary Jane scooted in beside him, cradling his head in her arms. Jeff crawled in behind the wheel, stepped on the starter, and the motor leaped into life. He slammed the truck into gear, and it shot out of the parking space.

An airplane roared low overhead, and the truck lurched wildly as bullets from its strafing guns slammed into the right front fender. Jeff wrestled the wheel and brought it back under control. He skidded around a corner and then slammed on the brakes hard. A yawning bomb crater in the pavement completely blocked the road ahead.

The plane came back for another strafing run on the stalled truck. This time the *Zero's* slugs missed their target by inches.

Jeff threw the gears into reverse, turned around, and made a turn to the right.

"Honey," he said, "things are getting too hot around here. I'll take you out to Wheeler with me, and you can phone your mother from there—if any phones are still working. Besides, there'll be nurses to look after our friend here."

The truck raced up the road, past the last of the houses and buildings and out through the fields of tall, green cane that lined it on either side.

The broad, flat fields, with their cane stalks waving back and forth in the gentle breeze, were a strangely peaceful contrast to the raging battle in the harbor. But up ahead, to the north, great pillars of black smoke billowed upward from Wheeler Field and Schofield Barracks, and the air above them was alive with Jap planes screaming in toward the harbor for the kill.

Twice more the pilots of *Zero* fighters, seeing the lone vehicle speeding up the road, dived at it with blazing guns. But both times, by a miracle, they missed the fast-moving target.

Jeff held his foot down hard on the accelerator. The truck flew up the deserted road trailing a cloud of dust.

The roar of an airplane blasted upon them from behind. It was more a scream than a roar, the sound of wind whistling and whining over wings and fuselage. Its dark shape flashed past low over their heads. Mary Jane could see the white U. S. star on the underside of the plane's wings.

The plane appeared to be out of control. Its wings wobbled crazily, like a bird that has been hit in flight, and a spiral of smoke trailed underneath it.

"Jeff!" Mary Jane cried. "That's one of ours!"

The Army P-40 grazed the top of the cane stalks, tried to pull up, dragged a wing-tip through the waving cane and then dropped into it. The thick growth seemed to provide a cushion for the skidding plane. It plowed along for a hundred yards and then rocked to a jolting stop, almost at the road's edge.

Jeff raced to the spot where the smoking plane lay and slammed on the brakes. He jumped out of the truck and ran over to the fighter, Mary Jane racing after him.

Inside the canopy, the pilot was slumped over the control stick. The windshield in front of him was shattered, and the back of his leather flight jacket was soaked with blood.

Jeff scrambled up on the wing and tugged at the plexiglass canopy. It had been hit in a dozen places by Jap machine-gun fire and was jammed shut.

"No wonder the poor guy couldn't get it open," Jeff muttered.

After a struggle, the canopy gave way and Jeff managed to slide it back. He reached in and unfastened the flier's safety belt. Then he dragged him out of the cockpit and slid his inert body down over the trailing edge of the P-40's wing.

Mary Jane was standing on the ground underneath. She reached up to grasp the wounded man's legs.

"Ease him to the ground, honey, if you can," Jeff said. "It looks like he's hurt pretty bad."

Mary Jane tried to hold the heavy body as it slid toward her. But the flier's weight was too much. The two slumped to the ground together.

Jeff jumped down off the wing and grasped the man under the arms.

"Don't worry, Janie," he managed to grin. "If the Japs couldn't kill him, we won't."

He dragged the man the short distance to the truck and put him into the seat beside the wounded sailor.

"It looks like you and I are a two-men ambulance corps today," he said, smiling to make Mary Jane feel better.

He stepped on the starter, and the truck hurtled on up the road toward Wheeler Field.

Jeff roared through the gates of Wheeler, unguarded now by the usual sentry, and screeched to a stop in front of a partly wrecked and still smoking hangar.

The destruction of the airfield was almost complete. It was even worse, if such a thing could be possible, than the shambles they had left behind at Pearl.

An hour earlier, the sleek Army fighters and bombers had been neatly lined up on the concrete airstrip wing-tip to wing-tip, their insignia flashing proudly in the sunlight. Now, like the ships in the harbor, they were twisted heaps of junk. Among the piled-up wreckage was the remains of a Japanese *Val* dive-bomber, the Rising Sun on the tip of its wing sticking up grotesquely in the air.

One Army P-40, its tail-section shot away, had been dragged around by a gun crew who were using its cockpit as a machine-gun mount.

Jeff dragged the unconscious sailor out of the seat and, with Mary Jane following at his heels, hurried him into the shelter of the open hangar door. Inside, three nurses had set up an emergency hospital and were treating about two dozen wounded airmen.

"Here," Jeff said, easing the man down on a

pile of blankets, "I've got another one for you. And there's one more outside."

He went out and returned in a moment with the injured flier.

The man nearest the door lay propped against the wall, his right shoulder wrapped in a blood-stained bandage.

"Hey, Jeff," he called. "I didn't recognize you under all that dirt."

"You're not so easy to recognize either, Slim," Jeff replied.

He knelt beside him. "What happened up here? I got caught out in the middle of the harbor when the first wave came over."

"Got a cigarette, chum?" Slim asked.

Jeff lit one and placed it between the wounded man's lips.

"Thanks." Slim took a deep drag of the fragment smoke.

"They really clobbered us good," he said. "I was in the mess hall having a bite of breakfast when all of a sudden the bombs started dropping. They sure enough caught us with our flaps down. Most of the ships weren't gassed. They didn't have ammo. And they were parked so close together, we didn't have a chance.

"I tried to take off after the first flight hit us. I managed to work my ship out into the open and was just starting to gun her down the strip when something hit me like a ton of bricks. The next thing I knew I was lying in here trussed up like a Christmas turkey. Some war I've had! I'm out of it before it gets good and started!"

One of the nurses bent over the wounded man.

"Don't worry, Lieutenant," she said. "That shoulder's not too bad. You'll live to fight again, as the poet says."

"Look, nurse," Jeff said. "I'm going to try and find me an operable airplane, if they haven't all been shot to pieces. Will you look after this little girl here? She's Commander Fisher's—"

Jeff looked around, but Mary Jane was nowhere in sight.

"That child can take care of herself." The nurse smiled. "While you two have been gabbing, she's been pitching in and helping. And believe me," she added emphatically, "we can use all the help we can get."

Just then Mary Jane walked past, carrying a pan of hot water. She put it down beside a wounded airman and began to wash the dirt and grime from his face.

"I guess she'll do," Jeff said.

The nurse's khaki uniform was dirty and smoke-stained. Her eyes were red-rimmed and bloodshot, and her face was streaked as though she had been crying.

"She'll do, all right," the nurse said as she left them. "She's a real little Army brat."

"Navy brat," Jeff corrected her.

From far off to the south, the steady booming of the explosions in Pearl Harbor echoed up the valley.

A Jap plane zoomed over the air-strip outside,

its nose-guns spitting viciously as it came. A clatter of machine-gun fire burst from the roof of an adjoining building, and the gun mounted on the wrecked P-40 opened up with a staccato hammering.

There was a tremendous blast and a flash of fire as the *Zero* crashed into the runway and skidded along the concrete, rolling crazily over and over like a flaming fire-ball.

"There's one that won't get away," Jeff said.

"Wait'll I get back up there behind a gun," Slim said, straining around to look through the door at the burning *Zero*. "I figure they owe me about twenty of those babies."

Jeff slapped him on his good shoulder and got to his feet.

"Okay, Slim," he promised. "If there's anything left around here fit to fly, I'll get you one or two to start you out."

He ran for the door. Over his shoulder he could see Mary Jane's slender figure bustling around the big room, busy at her job of helping the overworked nurses. When she saw him, she raised her right hand, put her thumb and forefinger together, and waved it at him in the good-luck sign of the Army Air Corps.

CHAPTER FIVE

Jeff Gets into the Air

AT A hangar at the far end of the field, Jeff found his crew-chief, Sergeant Murphy.

"Lieutenant boy," Murph said, "I sure am glad to see you."

Sergeant Murphy was scarcely more than five feet tall and weighed something better than two hundred pounds. Jeff had often wondered how he was able to scramble up and down the ladders that mechanics needed to service a fighter plane, much less squeeze his bulk into a fighter's cockpit. But somehow Murph managed to do it, and all the pilots agreed that he was the best crew-chief on the base.

"I figured you were going to show up sooner or later," Sergeant Murphy said. "And I've got an airplane for you. She was in the hangar, under repairs, and she's practically all in one piece. I gassed her up and filled her ammo belts. Wait just a minute."

Murph disappeared into the hangar, and in a few minutes the throaty roar of a powerful P-40 engine came throbbing through the open doors. Then the slim little sharp-nosed ship slid out of the cavernous building and onto the concrete strip. Murph was wedged into the pilot's seat. He gunned the motor once, let it idle down, squeezed his round body out of the cockpit, and climbed down to the ground.

"She's all yours, Lieutenant," he said. "Go get yourself a few."

As Jeff started to climb into the plane, Murph stopped him with a slap on the back. He pointed to Jeff's sneakers.

"You know, Lieutenant," he said, "according to the Geneva Convention rules of war, an officer is supposed to be in regulation uniform when he goes into battle. Those sneakers don't look very regulation to me."

"Well, I'll tell you something, Sergeant," Jeff replied. "According to the Geneva Convention, people are supposed to declare war before they start shooting. Does that make my sneakers okay?"

The sergeant held out his hand.

"It makes them okay with me, sir."

"Just for now," Jeff said, "under the circumstances, as you might say, my name is Jeff."

The sergeant grinned and shook Jeff's outstretched hand.

"Good luck, Jeff. And good hunting."

"Thanks, Murph," Jeff said. "I'll see if I can put your name on one."

Jeff strapped himself into his parachute, fastened his safety belt, and closed the plexiglass canopy over his head. In his rear-view mirror, he could see another formation of *Zeros* coming in for a pass at the field.

He gunned his engine, roared down the strip, and pulled his ship up into the air. The Jap planes were just behind him, only seconds out of machine-gun range.

Jeff stood the P-40 on her tail and headed for the blue. "Man," he thought prayerfully, "I hope Murph had this engine good and hot."

Murph had. The fighter bored straight up, reaching for the top of the sky like a homesick angel. Jeff flipped her over the top of a loop, and when he was right side up again, found himself on the tail of the Jap formation. A *Zero* was sitting square in his gunsights. He squeezed the trigger on the handle of his control stick, and the Jap took the full impact of his fire amidships. Jeff's

tracers plowed into the squat airplane, and it exploded in a flash of fire, scattering pieces of itself all around the pursuing P-40.

Jeff corrected his course and fastened onto the tail of another Jap. Instead of blowing up under the fire from Jeff's guns, the tracers produced a trailing stream of smoke and the *Zero* fell off on one wing. It spiraled down out of formation and crashed into a cane field.

"Okay, Slim," Jeff muttered under his breath. "There's one for you and one for Murph. Now how about a couple for myself?"

By this time he was over Pearl Harbor. The sight down below looked even more appalling than it had from the deck of the *Mister Mike*. Under the heavy curtain of smoke that covered them, all the battlewagons in Battleship Row seemed to be in a sunken or sinking condition.

Cruisers, destroyers, and tenders were capsized, sinking or burning.

The battleship, *Pennsylvania,* in dry dock at the Naval Station, was sitting there helplessly, taking a tremendous plastering. One of the destroyers ahead of her had capsized and lay, burning and smoking, on its side.

Across Ford Island, Jeff could see the old bat-

*Jeff corrected his course and fastened onto the tail
of another Jap plane*

tleship *Utah,* recently converted into a target ship, turned over and lying bottom up. All around her the water was littered with floating debris and swimming men.

Only the *Nevada* was moving, laboriously work- ing her way down the channel under heavy fire from group after group of strafing planes and dive- bombers.

As far as he could tell, Jeff was the only Ameri- can pilot in the air. Heedless of the firing from the Jap planes, he dove for the formation that was pounding the *Nevada* and opened up his guns. The *Val* dive-bomber in his gunsight exploded when he squeezed his trigger. A second *Val* winged over and crashed into the Navy Yard seaplane landing.

A thought hammered through his head. *These Jap planes aren't armored! When you hit them, they're done for!*

At that instant, a stream of bullets laced across his starboard wing. The P-40 staggered, then righted itself.

Jeff pulled up in a tight turn to shake off his at- tacker. The *Zero* turned even tighter than he did, and clung to his tail like a bulldog to the nose of a bull. Jeff tried another turn. When he came out of it, the Jap was still there, pouring slugs into him. The instruments in his cockpit shattered in a shower of glass. The canopy over his head was riddled.

The Air Corps was learning the hard way! Despite their lack of armor—or maybe because of it! —these Japanese *Zeros* were the finest fighting airplanes in the world!

He hoped he'd get down safely to tell that to the Brass. Everybody sure had underestimated these little pilots from Nippon!

Jeff dived sharply, then pulled up and flipped his plane into a wing-over. The Jap on his tail stayed right with him, pouring out a devastating fire. A slug hit the motor in what must have been a vital spot. It spat, coughed, sputtered, and died. A thin stream of smoke spiraled backward from the cowling, followed by a spurt of flame.

The hardest thing for a fighting man to admit is the fact that he has been whipped. Jeff yanked at the throttle, but the dead engine refused to respond. The fire from the burning motor came sweeping back toward the cockpit. *Anyway,* he consoled himself, *I got four of them before they got me!*

He pulled back the shattered cockpit canopy.

Jeff found himself floating slowly downward

Fortunately, the Jap's slugs hadn't jammed it. He unhooked his seat belt, felt to make sure that his parachute fastenings were secure, stood up, flipped the P-40 on its side, and dived overboard.

He counted *one, two, three,* then pulled the ripcord at his chest. The 'chute opened with a spine-twisting jerk, and Jeff found himself floating slowly downward, swaying back and forth like a child in a garden swing, three thousand feet above the smoking, burning horror-pit that was Pearl Harbor, graveyard of the United States Navy.

Below him, he saw his P-40 spiral down like a falling leaf, trailing a long streamer of smoke, and crash into the water.

A gentle wind pushed his 'chute northward. He drifted over the burning ships, over the smoldering wreckage of the Navy Yard, past row after row of houses on the base, over the streets of Pearl City, and finally out into the countryside.

He landed in a cane field.

Climbing out of his 'chute, he ran toward the road. If any cars were moving, he could hitch a ride back to Wheeler!

CHAPTER SIX

The Hospital Is Hit

JEFF fought his way through the tangle of tall cane to the roadway, just as an Army jeep came bouncing around a bend. The driver kicked up a small cloud of dust as he skidded to a stop. Jeff recognized him as a mechanic from Wheeler Field.

"Hi, Lieutenant," he said as Jeff climbed into the front seat beside him and the jeep jolted forward again. "What are you doing way out here?"

Jeff pointed upward at a cloud that floated past overhead.

"I just came from up there. By parachute. I tangled with a Jap, and he shot me down."

"What?" The boy's eyes went wide. "You mean to tell me those little slant-eyes can see straight enough to shoot anybody down? Especially the hottest pilot in the 16th?"

"They had us all fooled," Jeff said. "But I found out something. Those little fighters of theirs can fly rings around any airplane the Army's got. Or the Navy either, for that matter."

"They sure are clobbering the ships at Pearl," the driver said, shaking his head as though he couldn't believe what he had seen. "I just came past there. When the shooting started, I was down at Waikiki taking an early morning swim for myself. Figured I'd be needed at the field, so I borrowed this jeep. It was parked on the street with the keys in it. Figured whoever had checked it out wouldn't miss it in all the excitement."

"I'm afraid there's not enough left of the field to worry about," Jeff said. "They clobbered Wheeler even worse than Pearl. As far as I know, I took off the last fighter that could fly."

"Ho-ly smoke, Lieutenant! Are you kidding? We had three squadrons there yesterday."

"Well, we sure haven't got 'em now. Except scattered in pieces all over the runway. I'm going

back on the off-chance that Murph can patch together another P-40 for me."

"I hate to admit it," the soldier agreed, "but if anybody can do it, Murph can. I just hope I stay in the Air Corps long enough to know as much about airplanes as he does."

Jeff grinned. "After what's happened this morning," he said, "something tells me you're going to be in the Air Corps a long time."

They rolled through the gates of Wheeler and up the drive to the blasted air-strip.

At that instant, the guns on the tailless P-40 parked on the runway began to bark. A single Jap

Val whined down in a slanting dive, its whirling propeller aimed directly at the hangar the nurses had turned into a hospital. At a hundred feet, the pilot released his bomb. Then he zoomed sharply up and wheeled northward toward the mountains of Waialua.

The bomb went through the roof of the hangar and exploded with a roar like a firecracker in a tin can magnified a million times. Before Jeff's horrified eyes, the sides of the hangar collapsed inwardly, and a great column of smoke billowed skyward.

The tires screeched as the driver jammed on the brakes, and the jeep stopped with a jolt.

Jeff jumped out and started running for the smoking wreck of the building.

"Come on!" he yelled. "That place is full of wounded men!"

He didn't dare remind himself out loud that Mary Jane was in there too!

CHAPTER SEVEN

"A Real Little Navy Brat"

A HEAVY pall of smoke and dust obscured the inside of the hangar as Jeff and the sergeant shouldered their way through what remained of the door. Rafters and timbers and window frames were piled in smoking heaps like twigs on a bonfire, and from underneath came the whimperings and moans of wounded men.

"Mary Jane!" Jeff called frantically. "Mary Jane! Can you hear me?" When no answer came he cupped his hands to his mouth and yelled: "Ma-ry Ja-a-ane!"

Out of the smoke and dust a little figure stumbled to his side and grasped his hand.

"Oh, Jeff!" Mary Jane's voice was trembling. "Oh, Jeff, I'm so glad you're here."

Her face was streaked and dirty, and a thin trickle of blood ran down across her nose from a cut in her forehead.

Jeff took her in his arms.

"Are you all right, honey?"

"I'm fine, Jeff," she said. "But all these others . . ." She buried her head for a moment against his chest. "I was down at the other end of the hangar getting water from the tap when the bomb hit. It *was* a bomb, wasn't it, Jeff?"

"It was a bomb all right." Jeff choked up. "And I'd like to get my gunsights on the—"

Mary Jane pushed herself away from him.

"We've got to hurry. We've got to get those people out of there." She began to tug at the boards and beams that protruded from the piles of rubble.

"Sergeant!" Jeff yelled at the mechanic who had been driving the jeep. "Drive down to the other hangars on the double and get as many men as you can find to help out here."

"They're on their way, Lieutenant," the sergeant said. "They started coming when they saw the bomb hit."

As he spoke, a dozen men came streaming into the wrecked hangar, panting from their run across the field and choking on the smoke.

"Start clearing this away," Jeff ordered. But the men had already begun to dig into the piles of rubble.

The first form they removed was that of one of the nurses. Her face was blood-stained, and an arm dangled limp and crooked at her side. But when the men laid her gently down in a clear space on the concrete floor and Mary Jane began to sponge off her bloody and smoke-dirtied face, she opened her eyes and managed a feeble smile.

"It's up to you now, Janie," she said. Then her eyes closed again and her head lay limply in Mary Jane's lap.

Now the fast-working rescuers were laying out the survivors row on row. The two other nurses were among them, and Mary Jane realized with a shock that she was the only woman in the stricken building. She thought of her classes in First Aid, and hoped desperately that she would remember the right things to do.

"Soldier!" she called.

One of the men working on the rubble pile turned around.

"Yes, ma'am," he said instinctively.

"Get two small pieces of wood and tie this nurse's arm securely." Without knowing why she was doing it, except that it seemed to be natural work for a woman, Mary Jane found herself taking charge of the rescue operation. "Don't try to set the bone. We'll leave that for the doctor. Just make sure the arm is protected."

She moved to the soldier lying next to the nurse. His shirt had been torn away by the explosion, and a dark, ugly pool of blood was oozing from a deep wound in the muscles of his chest.

She looked up at the sound of Jeff's voice.

"I've told off these six men to help you, honey. Just tell them what you want them to do."

The wounded boy was writhing in the blankets that covered him, crying softly and turning his head from side to side.

"Hand me that kit, please," Mary Jane said. A soldier retrieved a white tin box, marked with a red cross, that lay under a fallen timber. Mary Jane opened it and took out a small glass syringe labeled: Morphine. She placed the point of the needle against the bulging muscle of the wounded man's arm. Her forehead broke out in an ice-cold sweat and her hand trembled.

"Come on, Jane," she said to herself. "You're a big girl now." She steadied her hand, closed her eyes, and plunged the needle deep into the flesh.

The soldier sighed deeply and lay quiet.

"Good work, Janie." It was the voice of the nurse with the broken arm, who had regained consciousness once more. In spite of the fact that her arm must have been hurting fearfully, she smiled a weak smile of encouragement. "You're doing fine. Keep it up!"

With the men to help her, Mary Jane worked her way down the grim rows of the wounded. She gave her orders coolly and quickly, and the soldiers jumped to do as she asked.

Once she came to a quiet form stretched out pitifully under a blanket. One look at his still face told her there was nothing she could do. The tears welled from her eyes as she pulled up the edge of the blanket and turned away.

Then she went on to the next man.

A rubber tourniquet to stop the flow of blood was tied to the boy's upper arm, and a needle, attached to a length of rubber tubing, was stuck into the big vein inside his elbow. The tubing trailed its end on the floor.

Mary Jane suddenly remembered. This was the boy who had been about to get a transfusion of blood plasma when the bomb fell! She had been watching the nurses getting ready to give it to him when they sent her to the tap for water. Her heart jumped up into her throat. Was he still alive?

She felt the pulse in his wrist that was lying stretched out at his side. There was a faint flutter of life, but his face was as still as a statue, and she had to put her ear over his mouth to know that he was still breathing.

He had to have blood! There was no mistake about that. But where was it to come from?

Mary Jane went quickly to the nurse with the broken arm.

"Janie," the nurse said, "I hate to tell you this. But what few bottles of blood plasma we had were smashed by the bomb explosion. I'm afraid there's nothing we can do unless . . ."

"Unless what?" Mary Jane asked as the nurse paused in the middle of her sentence.

"Unless you can give him a direct blood transfusion. Look, Janie, do you think you can try?"

Mary Jane felt herself curl up inside. She'd never expected anything like this. All of a sudden her hands were shaking, but she made herself speak. "You—you just tell me what to do, ma'am," she stammered, "and the boys and I will try."

The nurse made her injured arm, bundled up now in a makeshift splint, as easy as possible and struggled to a sitting position. Mary Jane rolled up a blanket and put it behind her back.

"Look at his dog tag," the nurse said. "See what type of blood he has."

Mary Jane reached into the open collar of the boy's shirt and pulled out the metal disk that hung around his neck on a chain.

"Type A positive," she reported.

"Good," the nurse said. "That's common. Now we need a donor with either type A or O."

One of the soldiers who had been helping Mary Jane was listening.

"Ma'am," he said, "my blood's A positive."

The nurse patted Mary Jane on the arm. "This is going to be hard on you, Janie. But the first time I saw you I said you were a real little Army—I mean Navy—brat.

"Now," she went on, speaking to the soldier who had volunteered to give his blood, "let's get busy. I suppose all the equipment is smashed, so we'll have to make it up as we go along. First, you'll have to be higher than he is, so the blood can flow downhill. See if you can rig some kind of a bed for yourself, about two feet higher than the floor."

The soldier began piling up pieces of timber to

form a sort of a rude cot beside the unconscious man.

"Now, Janie, you scout around and see if you can find two more syringes and a longer length of rubber tubing. Oh, and some alcohol."

Mary Jane scurried around in the debris until she had collected all the things the nurse asked for. Nearly all of the medical supplies had been blown to bits, but in one metal box she finally found a bottle of alcohol that hadn't been broken.

Meanwhile the soldier had completed his high bed of boards and stretched a blanket over it. Then he took off his shirt and lay down.

Working under the nurse's direction, Mary Jane broke off the glass needles of two syringes and joined them with a long length of sterile rubber tubing. She pulled out the needle that had been dangling from the wounded man's arm, adjusted the tourniquet, swabbed the vein with alcohol, and inserted the sterile needle that she had fastened to one end of the rubber tubing. Then she secured it with a piece of adhesive tape.

The nurse had been watching every move.

"Good work, Janie," she said approvingly. "We'll make an Army nurse out of you yet. Now, soldier," she said to the man lying on the pile of

boards, "make a fist while Janie applies a tourniquet to your arm."

The veins in the crook of the man's elbow stood
out big and blue. Mary Jane selected the biggest
one, sterilized it with alcohol and, as gently as she
could, jabbed in the needle. She had to make two
tries before it was firmly affixed in the vein and
she saw the soldier's eyes involuntarily blink at her
clumsy efforts.

"Oh, I hurt you," she blurted. "Oh, I'm so aw-
fully sorry."

The big soldier grinned. "What?" he said. "I didn't feel a thing."

Now the arms of the two men were connected by the rubber tube, the big soldier's about two feet higher than that of the white-faced man on the floor.

"All right, Janie," the nurse instructed, "remove the tourniquets.

"Now, soldier," she went on, "pump with your fist to help that blood along. We've got no way of measuring, so we'll just have to guess when you've given him enough."

Kneeling on the floor beside the man who was getting the blood, Mary Jane gently swabbed the boy's face with a cool, damp cloth.

The minutes went by, just how many Mary Jane had no way of knowing. Her own blood was pounding in her temples and she had to try hard to keep her hands from shaking.

But slowly, very slowly, color began to come back into the unconscious boy's dead-white face.

After what seemed like an eternity, the nurse spoke again.

"All right," she said. "That ought to do it."

Mary Jane removed the needle from the arm of the big soldier and covered the wound with a piece of tape. Then she did the same for the boy lying on the floor. The sting of the alcohol as she swabbed off the wound, caused his eyes to flutter open. He smiled weakly, then closed them again.

Mary Jane got to her feet. Suddenly all the strength seemed to drain out of her knees. There was a horrible emptiness in the pit of her stomach. The room swirled around her head with an angry roar and she pitched forward.

She felt herself being caught by a pair of strong arms and she clung desperately to them until her head cleared and she was strong enough to stand. Then she saw that it was Jeff who was holding her.

Quietly, she began to cry. Jeff held her tight and stroked her hair with his hand.

"I was watching you, honey," he said softly. "You were wonderful."

"You bet she was," the nurse said, smiling. "She did that like a professional."

"She can nurse me any time I get hit," put in the big soldier who had given the blood. "Any time at all." And he reached over and gave her a clumsy pat on the top of her dark hair.

As her head cleared and the strength flowed back into her legs, Mary Jane realized that the dull *boom-boom-boom* of the bombs bursting on

"I was watching you, honey," he said softly.
"You were wonderful."

Pearl Harbor had all but stopped. Instead of the continuous roar of sound that had been thundering up the valley, there was now only an occasional solitary and distant blast.

"Listen!" she said excitedly. "I think they've quit."

"It's been slacking off for quite a while," Jeff said. "You just haven't had time to notice it."

"I reckon they went home for more bombs," the soldier said. "But they'll be back."

"Yes," Jeff agreed. "I'm afraid that's one thing we can count on. They'll be back all right. You men stick around here until I can get some medical corpsmen to come and take over."

With his arm around her small, trembling shoulders, Jeff led Mary Jane out into the sunshine. For the first time since early morning, the blue sky above them was clear of enemy planes.

"Maybe they'll give us a breather," he said, "long enough for me to get you home where you belong."

CHAPTER EIGHT

"You Ought to Be in the Navy!"

THE water of the harbor was covered with a thick, black scum of oil as Mike steered his little boat toward the swimming men who had spilled out of the overturned launch. He looked back and caught one final glimpse of Mary Jane and Jeff running for the street, Jeff staggering under the weight of the wounded man he carried over his shoulder.

The sailor who had yelled: "Wait for me!" and then leaped into the boat beside him, was busily untangling a long length of line that had been part of the *Mister Mike's* smart rigging only a short time before.

"Welcome aboard, sailor," Mike said, shouting over the din of the bomb explosions.

"Just call me Pete," the sailor shouted back. "Say, kid, you ought to be in the Navy."

"That's what my dad says," Mike said. "Maybe you know him, Captain Morrison."

"Know him!" Pete exclaimed. "I'll say I know him! I served with the captain when he was skipper of the old *Wahelo* gunboat, out in the China Sea. We had a little trouble with the Japs out there too. So you're the skipper's kid? Well, how about that?"

As he talked, Pete was tying knots, about three feet apart, in the line. He secured one end firmly around the stump of the shattered mast.

"Now here's the ticket," he said. "There's a lot more men out there than we can haul aboard this little craft. We'll take on any that are badly hurt and drag the others in with this line."

Mike cut the engine to idling speed as they approached the area where the men were floundering in the water. Pete threw out the line and shouted instructions to the swimming men.

Their heads and arms and bodies were covered with a black coating of oil, but some of them flashed white teeth in a thankful grin as they took good grips on the knotted line that trailed astern of the little sailboat.

[*81*]

Only one man was badly injured. He was wearing a life jacket and two swimming men were holding his head up out of the water. Mike and Pete had difficulty pulling him on board without hurting him even more.

They carefully laid him down in the cockpit of the *Mister Mike,* and Pete wrapped him in a torn piece of sail.

Mike circled round and round the area, peering through the smoke and haze for more survivors. The men hanging onto the knotted line trailed after the boat like the bits of newspaper that dangle on the end of a kite's tail.

One man's greasy hands slipped from the rope. A shout went up from the others, and Mike brought the boat around in a wide circle to pick him up again.

"Nice work, skipper," Pete said. "You take after your old man."

All around them, the bombs kept showering their rain of death on the ships in the harbor. A small ship off to their left took a direct hit and blew up like a Roman candle. The water astern of

them came alive with the splashes made by the fragments of torn metal. Mike looked back. One of the men who had been hanging onto the rope was gone. There was no sign of him. Mike kept on his course to the dock.

Pete yelled: "Look out, skipper!"

Another kill-crazy *Zero* came down at them from astern in a whistling dive. At almost deck level, he opened up his guns. The slugs smashed in among the men in the water and Mike saw two more of them disappear under the oily surface.

For the second time that morning, a line of machine-gun bullets hammered across the deck of the little sloop. This time, they caught her square amidships, throwing up a shower of splinters within inches of Mike's hand. The *Mister Mike* staggered and began to sink low in the water as the black, oily sea gurgled into her hull through the shot-holes in her bottom.

Pete was down on his knees, clutching at his shoulder. His shirt was glistening red with blood.

"I'll make it, skipper," Pete said. "But you'd better pour on the coal. We're going down fast."

Mike turned toward the men hanging onto the stern rope and made a megaphone of his hands.

"Hang on, men!" he shouted. "Hang on good

and tight! I've got to speed her up before we sink!"

He advanced the throttle, and the sluggish little boat, now more than half filled with scummy water, shook herself and picked up speed.

On the knotted rope that trailed astern, the rescued men clung for dear life.

The *Mister Mike* sagged lower and lower in the water. Her forward speed slowed to a crawl. As her bow nudged the piling of the Navy Yard dock, her gunwales were barely out of the water. Mike made a grab for the ladder, and a hand reached down to help him. He saw that other men were scrambling down the sides of the dock, or throwing lines to the oil-soaked survivors still in the water.

Standing on top of the dock at last, he looked down at his boat.

Water was filling up the cockpit and washing over the deck timbers. Then the hull sank beneath the surface, and air bubbles gurgled up as the shattered stump of the little sloop's mast slid down and disappeared.

Mike gulped to choke back a sob. For a moment he forgot about the bomb blasts and the fire and the diving planes. All he could think of was that his beautiful new boat had sunk. Like the big

"Too bad, skipper. She was a real nice little ship."

ships out in Battleship Row, the *Mister Mike* was gone. She hadn't had a chance.

"Too bad, skipper. She was a real nice little ship."

It was Pete, standing by his side, still clutching his torn and bleeding shoulder. "But she's got good company down there on the bottom. Just about the whole U. S. Navy."

As he spoke, Pete reeled like a drunken man and keeled over in a dead faint.

CHAPTER NINE

The "1010" Dock

THE dock on which Mike stood was a madhouse of fire, smoke, milling men, spitting machine guns and the overpowering roar of bomb explosions.

Cruisers and destroyers were tied up all around it. In the big drydock alongside, the battleship *Pennsylvania,* proud flagship of the Pacific Fleet, sat high and dry like a helpless fish out of water. Ahead of her lay a pair of destroyers.

Jap dive-bombers were pounding the ships unmercifully and smashing the dock installations.

The drydock had been emptied of water and its high sides rose up all around the ships, making it almost impossible to see. Nevertheless, the gunners on the decks were putting up a courageous fight, pumping a steady stream of antiaircraft fire into the oncoming planes. But the Japs poured in relentlessly through the deadly curtain of steel.

A giant traveling crane, used for lifting heavy material from the dock to the decks of the ships under repair, stood on rails that ran along the dock's edge. Mike stared fascinated as he watched the operator run the huge machine back and forth along the rails in a futile attempt to frighten off the low-flying bombers, like a mother hen trying frantically to protect her brood of chicks.

"There's a good man to have on our side," Mike said to himself. But the thought had no sooner occurred to him than a bomb hit the crane and toppled it over in a spiraling cloud of smoke and dust.

"Hey!" Mike hailed a pair of sailors who were going by on the double. "How about giving me a hand with my buddy?"

The sailors stopped and stared at Mike and the fallen Pete in amazement.

"Say, this is no place for a kid," one of them said. "Sure, we'll take care of this guy and turn him over to the medics. But you'd better get out of here, son."

Gently the two men picked Pete up and disappeared with him into the swirling smoke.

"There goes another good man," Mike thought. He waved his hand. "So long, pal, and good luck!"

It was "So long and good luck" for an awful lot of good men this morning.

Now Jap bombers were diving in on the dock from every point of the compass. The *Pennsylvania* was their prime target, but the bombs that overshot her big bulk smashed into the two destroyers or the dock installations. In a matter of minutes, the two small ships were enveloped in a mass of flames. One of them caught a direct hit in her magazines, blew up with a mighty roar, showered the dock with a frightful rain of debris, and slowly rolled over and came to rest on her side.

Someone had thought to order the drydock flooded, and the rising water swirled and gurgled in eddies, its surface littered with a collection of floating junk.

Up to now, during a morning of steady bombardment and fire and deafening noise—a morning that seemed as if it had been going on forever and would never stop—Mike had been too busy to think much about himself. But standing here on the "1010" dock, with violent death screaming down out of the sky all around him, he suddenly realized that he was scared. Real scared! Much

more scared than he'd been on the *Mister Mike!*
He'd better get out of here!

Before he knew what he was doing, he found
himself running blindly across the dock through
the thick screen of smoke that coated the inside
of his nose and mouth with a bitter, acrid taste.

At the northern end of the dock, Mike came to a
gangplank stretched to the deck of a cruiser that
was tied up alongside. The name on the stern said:
New Orleans. On the deck, the crew was working
feverishly. Mike needed to be with somebody!
Anybody! Other people! He raced up the gangplank and onto the cruiser's deck.

The crew, he saw, had formed a human chain,
and were passing shells and bags of powder from
down inside the hold of the ship to the men who
were manning the guns. Mike crowded his way
into the line.

"What's going on?" he asked a big sailor, whose
face was streaked with smoke-blackened sweat.

"Power line's busted," the sailor grunted. "Got
to move this stuff by hand."

The sailor turned, took a bag of powder from
the man next to him, and pushed it into Mike's
hands. Mike swiveled and passed it on to the next
man in line.

Now he was doing something! He was working again! He was fighting back! The invisible hand that had been clutching at his stomach relaxed. His heart quit pounding in his throat. He forgot everything but the need to keep the powder moving.

A bomb exploded on the ship tied up next to the cruiser. Instinctively, all the men in the line ducked.

"Boy!" Mike thought. "If one ever hits this line of powder, there won't be enough left of us to pick up!"

He thought of his soft, safe bed up on the hill at Makalapa and wished that he could crawl into it and pull the covers up over his head to shut out the noise. But he kept on with the back-breaking job of keeping the human supply-chain going.

During a brief lull in the firing, a man appeared out of the pall of smoke, carrying a pail of water and a bag of apples and oranges. He went from man to man in the line, giving each one a drink from his tin dipper and offering them an apple or an orange to munch on. Mike saw that he wore the gold cross of a Navy chaplain on the grimy collar of his khaki shirt.

The chaplain smiled through his smoke-smudged face and said a word of encouragement to each man as he passed. When he held out a dipper of water to Mike, he looked down at the boy's costume of shorts and sneakers and shook his head.

"You look mighty young to be a sailor, son."

"Well, sir, I'm not," Mike replied. "This war sort of caught up with me."

"I guess it sort of caught up with all of us," the chaplain said. "Here, have a drink of water. It'll do you good."

Mike took a deep drink. The water tasted cool and sweet and cut the bitter film of smoke-taste in his mouth.

"Well, boys," the chaplain said as he moved on down the line with his pail of water and his fruit, "it looks like we're not going to have time for church this morning. So you'll just have to praise the Lord while you pass the ammunition."

Time dragged on endlessly. Mike's arms and shoulders ached, and the stinging smoke and fumes burned his eyes and made hot tears stream down his cheeks. The supply line rolled on without a stop. Turn, grab, wheel, shove. Turn, grab, wheel, shove. The men worked without speaking. They were too tired and too shocked to talk.

Mike was standing close to the ship's rail when the bomb struck. It hit the water midway between the cruiser and a supply ship berthed next to it, and exploded with a thunderous blast. The big ship lurched sickeningly under the impact of the near-miss.

Mike had just reached for a heavy powder bag and was holding it in his arms, bent over and off balance, when the deck fell away underneath him.

He struggled desperately to keep his feet, staggering backward like a lumberjack trying to stay upright on a rolling log. His legs hit the low rail and
he went overboard, kicking and clawing at the air
as he fell.

He landed flat on his back in the water. The
force of the fall knocked the breath from his body,
and everything went black.

CHAPTER TEN

Torpedo Boats in Action

THE shock of the chill water cleared Mike's head almost instantly. Coughing and choking, he bobbed to the surface and began swimming for the gray steel side of a ship that towered above him.

The luck that had protected him all during the battle stayed with him now. Two sailors on the ship's deck saw him struggling in the water. They threw him a line and pulled him up over the side.

Safe on the deck, Mike shook the water from his head and looked around. The swell set up by the exploding bomb had carried him to the supply ship. It was smaller than the cruiser, but the activity on board was just as furious. A long human chain was passing ammunition to the antiaircraft gunners who were firing as fast as they could load.

"Welcome aboard," one of the sailors said, grinning. "Where did you drop in from?"

Mike pointed to the cruiser.

"Over there," he said. "I fell off."

The sailor laughed.

"I don't blame you," he said. "If I was a better swimmer, I'd fall off too and head for shore. Things are a little too hot here to suit me."

"You can say that for me," the second sailor added. "But right now we'd better get over there and give those guys a hand before the chief starts yelling his head off."

"You've got something there," the first sailor said. "It's bad enough we've got a war on our hands, without having the chief lacing into us too."

With Mike following after them, they threaded their way past four big motor torpedo boats that were lashed to the deck.

"What are those things doing here?" Mike asked.

"We were getting ready to take them out to Manila," the sailor answered. "But they may never get there now."

In the bow of each of the motorboats was a 50-caliber machine gun. The guns were covered with canvas tarpaulins for protection against the weather, but their shapes under the canvas were unmistakable.

"Hey, hold it a minute!" Mike said. "Do you suppose those guns can be fired?"

The sailor clapped a hand to the top of his bare head.

"Holy mackerel!" he yelled. "Where have we been keeping our brains? Of course they can! Jim, you and the kid clear these guns for action while I go get the chief."

He sprinted across the deck.

Mike and Jim had the covers off all four guns by the time the sailor returned. He was accompanied by a chief petty officer and a dozen enlisted men. The men staggered under the weight of heavy ammunition boxes.

The chief, a tall, thin, wiry man, began barking out orders. In three minutes all of the guns on the MTB's were firing, adding their sharp, staccato hammering to the din that pounded all around them.

A "V" of Jap fighters swooped down at the deck, their nose guns spitting red flame as they came. The gunners on the MTB's set up a wild cheering as they threw a wall of fire at the diving planes. The firing was more enthusiastic than accurate. The Japs zoomed away unhurt.

Mike had been passing clips of ammunition to Jim, who was feeding the ammo into the gun the chief was firing.

"How about it, Chief?" Jim begged. "How about a turn on that gun?"

"Wait a minute," the chief said. "Keep your shirt on. There'll be plenty of action for all hands before this is over."

"Yeah, I know, Chief," Jim insisted. "But what about my kids?"

"You haven't got any kids," the chief said.

"Not now, I haven't. But someday I will. And what am I going to tell them I was doing on the day the war began? I want to be able to tell them all about how I knocked down a Jap."

"You just take it easy," the chief said, squinting up at the sky through the rings of the gunsight. "You just keep that ammo coming. You'll get your turn later. As soon as I get me a Jap, this baby's all yours."

"How about me, Chief?" Mike asked eagerly.

There was a lull in the firing, and the chief looked around. "What's this kid doing here?" he demanded. "How did he get on this ship?"

"We fished him out of the drink," Jim said. "And if anybody deserves a turn on that gun, he does. These MTB's were sitting all wrapped up like Christmas presents until the kid came along. He was the one who gave us the idea to break them out and use their guns."

"Well, now, you don't say!" the chief grinned. "You want a go at this chopper, sonny?"

Mike stepped forward.

"Now you hold these two handles here with both hands," the chief explained. "And when you want to fire, you press these triggers here. Get it?"

Mike nodded. He grasped the handles of the machine gun and swung it around on its swivel.

"Here they come!" the chief yelled. "Let them have it, kid!"

The "V" of *Zero* fighters had swung around and come back for another strafing run on the ships. This time, the advancing line of slugs stitched a pattern straight across the supply ship's deck. Everyone in the MTB's, except the men who were firing the guns, ducked. The bullets hit the gun on the number three boat and knocked it off its mounting. The sailor who was firing it slumped down to the deck.

Mike tried to keep the planes in the rings of his gun-sight

As the planes came in, Mike tried to keep them in the rings of his gun-sight. But, as he fired, he saw that his tracers were streaming far behind them. When the planes roared over for the second time, the chief grabbed the handles of the gun from Mike's hands.

"Son," he said, "you're wasting ammunition. You've got to lead them more. Shoot ahead of them and let them fly into your line of fire."

Another *Zero* came barreling down at the ship.

"Here," the chief said, "I'll show you."

The *Zero* flew squarely into the upbeating pattern of the tracers from the chief's gun. It burst into flames and hurtled over the deck, smashing into the water on the other side of the ship.

Another big cheer went up from the men on the MTB's.

The Jap pilot fought his way clear of the wreckage and bobbed to the surface, floating toward the side of the ship. A sailor threw him a line, and the man made a feeble grab for it. He missed, and then his heavy flying suit dragged him down. His upturned face was twisted with terror as it disappeared under the oily surface.

"These little motorboats are all right," the chief said, grinning and pounding Mike on the back.

"They don't even have to be in the water. You can fight 'em from a dry deck!"

The noise went on unceasingly. Pounding into Mike's ears. Hammering at his brain. The crashing of bombs, the shock of the 50-calibers, the dull reverberation of explosions from all over the harbor. Mike went back to his endless job of keeping the ammunition supply line moving, working like a robot, conscious of nothing but the dull routine of movement.

Then, almost as suddenly as it had started, the awful noise stopped. One minute it was battering against Mike's eardrums like surf beating up on a shore. The next minute there was silence, broken only by an occasional blast from the other side of the harbor.

The men in the ammunition line stopped, looked up, and slowly lowered the ammo boxes and powder bags to the deck. One by one they collapsed and sat down, holding their heads in their hands, dog-tired and bone-weary. Mike staggered to the ship's rail and down the gangplank to the dock. He looked back at the ship. She had taken a few scattered hits, but there was not much serious damage. Aside from the jumbled litter on her decks, she seemed to be in fairly good shape.

She still rode high and handsome in the water. And the Stars and Stripes flapped briskly in the morning breeze from her maintop and her stern.

Mike looked up. The sky was almost clear of planes. A few Japs still hovered around overhead, but they were flying high and seemed to be heading off toward the north, up over the mountains that towered their tall, green ridges above Pearl Harbor.

It looked as though the attack was over, at least for a little while. Mike glanced at his new watch. 10:15! It hardly seemed possible that it had been only a little more than two hours ago that he had seen the first bomb come whistling down out of the peaceful Sunday morning sky!

He stumbled on across the dock until he came to the stucco wall of a building. Leaning against it, he let his tired body slump down until he was sitting on the concrete pavement.

His chin dropped on his chest, and he closed his eyes and went to sleep.

CHAPTER ELEVEN

"The Japs Are Coming Back!"

A HAND roughly shaking his shoulder woke Mike up. It was a sailor, wearing the white armband of the Shore Patrol.

"I don't know what you're doing here, sonny, but you'd better get on home."

Mike jumped to his feet. He looked at his watch. Gosh! One o'clock! He'd been asleep more than two hours!

He realized that he must have been completely worn out to have slept through all the racket and commotion that were going on around him.

Gangs of sailors and civilian workers were using cranes, bulldozers, and tractors to clear away the wreckage of the dock. Men swarmed over the decks of every ship still afloat, clearing them for action. A human chain, like the one Mike had been a part of on the *New Orleans* passed bags of powder from the dock to the decks of ships that were still fit to fight.

Gun crews on board worked on their weapons, cleaning them, reassembling them, and firing an occasional burst to make sure they were ready for the attackers when they came back.

Billows of black smoke still rolled skyward from the hard-hit battleships in the harbor and the shore installations beyond them on Ford Island, but most of the fires seemed to have been brought under control.

A lone airplane appeared in the sky. From somewhere across the harbor a machine-gun opened up on it. The plane banked and the sun caught the glint of the blue circle and white star of the U. S. Navy under the wing. As abruptly as its clatter had started, the machine-gun stopped shooting.

"No wonder those gunners are ready to shoot up anything by this time," Mike thought.

As he made his way toward an exit gate, a sentry, carrying a rifle, stopped him.

"Where do you think you're going, kid?" His face was set in a grim scowl.

"Why—I—I—" Mike stammered. "I guess I'm just going home."

"Where's that?" the sentry snapped.

"Makalapa Heights," Mike answered. "You see, my dad—"

"Then what are you doing here? How did you get in?"

"I've been here since seven-thirty this morning," Mike said. "I got caught in the fight."

"*What?*" The sentry looked suspicious. "And where were you while the fireworks were going on?"

"Out in the harbor, most of the time," Mike replied. "Then I came in and helped the crew on the *New Orleans.*"

The sentry peered hard at Mike's face and hands and clothes, black and grimy with smoke and powder stains.

"Well, I'll be— Look, kid, you'd better get out of here before the Japs come back." He nodded toward the gate. "Go on. Beat it!"

"Do you really think the Japs are coming back?" Mike asked.

"Think?" the sailor said. "I know darn well they're coming back. You don't suppose they'd knock out the Navy like this and not come back and try to finish it off!"

"Then maybe I'd better stay here and help get ready for them," Mike said.

"Nothing doing, sonny," the sentry said sternly. He took Mike by the arm and marched him to the gate. "This is man's work. You go on home and tell your mother she wants you. Now, git!"

Mike walked out the gate and turned up the hill toward Makalapa Drive.

From the heights he could look down over the whole of Pearl Harbor. The sight made his stomach shrivel up inside him. The big battleships were all out of business—sunken, capsized, jammed in against the quays, or smoking piles of rubble. The harbor was littered with wrecked cruisers, destroyers, and smaller craft. The "1010" Dock and Ford Island were a shambles of twisted wreckage. Hickam Air Field was completely destroyed, the skeletons of fighters and bombers scattered all over its runways.

He turned into his own driveway and went into the dim coolness of the house. Here, at least, was one thing that hadn't changed since this morning!

His mother came running out of the kitchen and threw her arms around him.

"Oh, Mike! Mike! Mike!"

Her eyes were red-rimmed in a white face that looked suddenly old and tired. She clung to him, dug her head into his chest and sobbed, with dry eyes, as though she had run out of tears to cry.

"Oh, Mike! I didn't know where you were! It was awful! I was so afraid for you!"

Mike patted her gently on the shoulders.

"I'm okay, Mom. I didn't get hurt . . ."

He led her to the sofa and they sat down side by side, Mrs. Morrison still clutching Mike's hands in her own.

"Is Dad all right, Mom? Have you heard from him?"

"Yes, thank the good Lord, your father's safe. He managed to get a call through from his office just after the bombs stopped. But, Mike, you don't know how I worried—you and Jeff and your father all out somewhere in that terrible—"

"How about Jeff, Mom? Did he get in touch with you?"

"Yes, he was here. He's all right too."

Mike squeezed her hands. "Then quit worrying, Mom. It's all over. Everything's all right now."

Mrs. Morrison dabbed at her eyes with the hem of her apron, straightened up, and smiled.

"Look at me," she said. "Sitting here gabbing while you're probably starving to death."

Mike suddenly realized how hungry he was. He felt as if he hadn't eaten for a month.

"Come on out to the kitchen," his mother said, "and I'll fix you a plate of the chicken I was planning to have for lunch. I fed Jeff when he came in, but—"

"Did Jeff get Mary Jane home safe?"

"Yes, after it was all over. The poor little thing was as white as a sheet. Her mother took her home and gave her a hot bath and put her to bed."

"Where's Jeff now?" Mike asked, between mouthfuls of the hot chicken pie his mother had put on the table in front of him.

"He rushed in, gulped down some food just like you're doing—don't eat so fast, son, it won't get away from you—then he showered, put on a uniform, and hurried back to the field. He said the Japs would be back any time and everyone is alerted for twenty-four hour duty."

"That's what they're all saying," Mike agreed. "That the Japs are coming back."

"Your father says so too. He says if things stay quiet until evening, he may get home for supper. But he doesn't expect to."

While Mike ate, he told his mother what had happened to him that morning.

"And my brand-new boat, Mom. They sunk her. She was the prettiest little sailboat you ever saw, and they hammered her to pieces!"

"Don't fret," his mother said. "Just be thankful none of you was hurt. You can always get another sailboat."

She took the empty plate from the table and put it into the sink.

"Now you go right upstairs and take a hot shower and slip into bed. You look as if you could use a good, long nap."

"All right, Mom," Mike said and started up the stairs to his room.

He let his tired bones and muscles relax under the soothing massage of the steaming jets of water. Then he dried himself briskly with a towel, put on fresh clothes, and went back downstairs.

"I thought I told you to go to bed," his mother scolded.

"Mom, I just can't," Mike said seriously. "If the Japs are coming back—if Dad and Jeff have to be on duty—I just can't stay up here and twiddle my thumbs when there's so much to do."

"But what can *you* do, son?" his mother asked anxiously. "You're just a boy. Leave those things for the men. You'll be a man soon enough."

Mike shook his head. "No, Mom. There's plenty I can do. I can help down at the Navy Yard. I helped them there this morning. Gosh, Mom," he blurted, "I'm almost as big as Jeff."

Mrs. Morrison looked at this tall, young boy of hers.

[*113*]

"I've tried to think war wouldn't come, Mike," she said sadly. "But I couldn't wish it away. It's here. And I guess men have to fight."

"Gee, thanks, Mom!" Mike kissed her on the cheek and bolted out the kitchen door.

At the Navy Yard gate—Mike had carefully

chosen another gate this time to avoid the sentry who had ordered him out—he again was stopped by the guard on duty.

"Nobody's allowed in here, son. Go peddle your papers."

"But I came to help," Mike protested. He pointed to a gang that was clearing away the rubble from the deck of a ship moored to the dock. "I can do that as well as a grown man. Please, sailor, I just want to help."

The guard, his nerves still raw from the experience of the morning, growled a reply.

"Look, kid, you're bothering me. Go away!"

A voice behind Mike spoke calmly.

"I wouldn't be too hasty, if I were you, sentry. This boy is a pretty good man to have around right now."

Mike wheeled. It was the chaplain from the *New Orleans* who had cheered the men on and told them to praise the Lord and pass the ammunition.

"I didn't recognize you there for a minute, son," he said. "Your face is a good deal cleaner than I remember it."

"Yes, sir," Mike said. He felt that the chaplain was an old friend. "I went home and changed

[*115*]

and then came back to see if I could help get ready for the Japs when they come back."

"That's the spirit, son," the chaplain said. "Sentry, this lad did a man's job on the *New Orleans* at the height of the attack. I think we need every man we can get. Pass him in. I'll take the responsibility."

"If you say so, sir," the sentry said, saluting.

"Thanks, sir," Mike said gratefully, and dashed across the open dock.

A sweating chief petty officer was directing a work gang—composed equally of Navy men and civilians—in disentangling a mass of cable that had been twisted together like a wad of thread by a bomb explosion.

"You want me to start clearing away that pile of stuff over there?" Mike asked him.

"Sure. Good idea," the C.P.O. said. "Hop to it." Then he glanced at Mike. "Say," he said, "where did you come from? This is no place for kids."

"Do you want that stuff cleared away or don't you, Chief?" Mike demanded.

The chief grinned. "I told you I did," he snapped. "Get hopping!"

As the men worked, they talked in panting grunts.

"You think they'll come back?"

"Sure they'll come back."

"And this time we'll be ready for them!"

"What with?"

"Sure, look at the Navy out there. We've got nothing to fight back with."

"Yeah, but what we've got will be ready for them. We sure weren't ready this morning."

"C'mon, give me a hand with this cable."

Every few minutes the men looked up and scanned the sky, as though waiting for the first sign of the returning Japanese raiders.

Mike worked steadily. The chief ignored the fact that he was a boy and snapped orders at him as impartially as he did to the other men.

A Navy commander, accompanied by a man in civilian dress, walked up to the C.P.O.

"Chief," he said, "we need some volunteers. The minecraft *Arapahoe* is capsized over near the sub base, and we've discovered that some of her men are trapped inside her hull. We're organizing a party to try to get them out, and we need some hands who know something about cutting equipment. Thought maybe some of your men might qualify."

"Just a minute," the chief said. He turned to the working party.

"Hold it!" he yelled. "Hold it a second."

Rapidly he told them the commander's story.

"Any of you men here know anything about acetylene torch work?"

Three men raised their hands.

"Okay, Commander," the chief said. "They're all yours. Now the rest of you men get back to work. On the double."

The men who had volunteered followed the commander as he turned and walked away.

Mike waited until the chief's head was turned. Then quietly he slipped away and joined the volunteers.

CHAPTER TWELVE

Underwater Death Trap

WHEN the party of volunteers reached the dockside, a Navy launch was waiting for them with five other men already on board.

"All right, men," the commander said. "Let's shove off."

He led the way down the ladder, and the men scrambled after him. Mike kept himself well in the background, out of the officer's sight.

The sailor at the helm gunned the engine, and the launch leaped away from the pier in a wide circle and cut through the dirty water of Pearl Harbor.

This morning, Mike remembered, the water in the harbor had been clean, blue-green, and sparkling in the sunlight. Now it was covered with a filthy film of oil and littered with all manner of floating flotsam, jetsam, and junk.

In a few minutes they came to the *Arapahoe*, which had been anchored near the small peninsula that jutted out around the submarine base.

The little minecraft had been hit hard and rolled completely over in the water. Her sharp bow jutted upward and her stern was submerged, with most of her barnacle-covered keel exposed to the air.

A man had been sitting on her broad hull waiting for them. Mike saw that he held a hammer in his hand. The helmsman cut the engine, and the

launch nosed carefully up to the sunken hulk.

"Are they still okay, Smith?" the commander called.

"Yes, sir," the sailor with the hammer replied. "They're all alive, but they say the air is getting awful bad."

The officer turned to the rescue party.

"Men," he said, "I'm Commander Mason. Now this is the story. We found out just a little while ago that there are men still alive in this ship. Smith has been talking to them in Morse code by rapping on the hull. How we're going to get to them I don't know. But Mr. Young here," he indi-

cated the civilian, "is a naval engineer and knows the insides of these vessels like the palm of his hand. So I'm going to throw the ball to him. Listen carefully and pay strict attention."

Mr. Young cleared his throat. He was a small man and looked as though he would be much more at home bending over a drawing board than directing a tough crew of sailors in a risky rescue operation. But he took charge coolly and efficiently.

"Where is the tapping coming from, Smith?" he asked the man on the hull.

Smith indicated a spot just back of the center of the hull.

"The tapping is pretty faint, isn't it?" the engineer inquired.

"Yes, sir. And I've had a hard time making them hear me."

Mr. Young reflected for a long moment, shaking his head and scratching the stubble of whiskers on his chin. Like most men in Honolulu, he hadn't time to shave this morning.

"I'd say they're in the forward engine room," he declared at last. "Now these men were lucky enough to be caught in a trapped bubble of air. Fortunately, it was big enough to keep them alive this long, but it can't last forever. So we've got to work fast."

The men of the rescue party listened attentively.

"As you know, Commander, this ship has a double bottom. Even if we had the time to cut through both layers of steel, we'd almost certainly find that the inner 'skin' is below the water level. That means their air supply would escape through the first hole our cutting torch made, and they'd drown long before we could get them out. So, under the circumstances, cutting our way to them won't work. We'll have to think of something else."

Mr. Young took a blueprint from his jacket pocket and studied it for several minutes silently. Then he spread it out on the launch's deck, and the men peered anxiously over his shoulder.

"This is a chart of the interior plan of a ship of this class. The trapped men are undoubtedly in this compartment here."

He traced his forefinger across the chart as he talked, to make his meaning clear.

"Now, between the men, here, and the port side of the hull, here, are these two large compartments. Both will be flooded, but they seem to offer the only means, if any, of getting to those men. These sections of the ship, on this side and on this, are a maze of small compartments. It's plain that the ship took a hit here and another one here. So these compartments are certain to be fouled up. That leaves us just one chance."

Mr. Young looked up from his study of the chart.

"Which one of you men is the diver?"

A tall, husky man stepped forward.

"I am, sir," he said.

"You've got your gear with you?"

"Yes, sir. Right here."

"All right, then," Mr. Young said. Again he pointed to the chart.

"You'll find a porthole right here. Luckily, the ship's slanted over a bit to starboard so it ought to be clear. When you get through it, swim over to this spot here. Take your bearings carefully before you start from the porthole, because it's going to be as dark as the inside of a coal mine down there, and your light won't help much at any distance. And you can't afford to waste any time getting lost. Got it so far?"

"Yes, sir." The diver nodded gravely.

"Good. Now, when you get to this point here, you'll find a watertight door that will be secured shut with heavy 'dogs' on your side. And don't forget, everything will be upside down. Undog it and then proceed across the second compartment to here. Here, you'll find another door that will be dogged on your side. And if the Lord is especially good to us, that door will lead into the compartment where the men are trapped."

As Mr. Young talked, the men had been listening, not saying a word, and every face glistened with sweat that was not caused alone by the heat of the sun. Mike felt himself hardly daring to breathe.

"Now just one more thing before you go," the engineer said. "Getting in to those men will be one thing. Getting them out will be quite another. You'll have oxygen and they won't, and they're already in a weakened condition.

"Take a light, strong line with you. We'll secure one end of it here, and when you get to the men, secure your end in there. Then they can follow the line out hand over hand."

Mr. Young looked up.

"It's a slim chance," he said, "a mighty slim

[*125*]

one. But as far as I can see, it's the only one they've got. All right, now you're on your own. Good luck!"

Two sailors helped the big diver adjust a rubber mask over his face and an air tank on his back. The mask covered his entire face. With its two big goggles over his eyes and the exhaling apparatus in front of his nose and mouth, it made him look like a monster from another world.

When his equipment was securely in place, and with the loop of the line draped over his shoulder, the diver slipped over the side and disappeared into the murky depths.

The men on the launch leaned over the rail and gazed into the water, following the trail of air bubbles that gurgled to the surface from the diver's mask.

Mike found himself gripping the rail hard with both hands. His heart beat wildly in his chest, and he realized that he was more tense and excited than he had been at any time during the raid.

A minute passed. Two. Five. Ten. The deck of the launch was as quiet as a church. The sailors stared silently at the uprushing bubbles like men in a trance.

Then the diver's head appeared on the surface,

and the men broke the tension with a wild yell.

The diver scrambled up the boat's ladder to the deck and ripped off his mask. He was panting, his face was dead white, and his hands shook uncontrollably.

"Sir!" he gasped. "Sir! I couldn't get through the porthole!" The big diver began to sob and buried his face in his hands.

Commander Mason jerked his hands down and shook him roughly.

"Here!" he barked. "Get hold of yourself, man! Now what's this all about?"

The diver seemed to regain some control of his nerves, although when he spoke it was in a series of panting gasps.

"Sir," he said, "I'm too big—too big to get through that porthole—found it all right, but couldn't get through—too big—even unstrapped my tank to drag it in after me—but I couldn't get through—too big—" The diver broke off his almost incoherent words with a sob.

Commander Mason wheeled around.

"Any of you men qualified as divers?" he snapped.

Mike stepped in front of the crowd of silent men.

"I am, sir," he said.

The commander noticed Mike for the first time. His jaw dropped.

"What are *you* doing here?" he roared.

"I came with the rescue party, sir," Mike explained. "I was working on the dock when you asked for volunteers."

"Then what in blazes were you doing *there?* Get back out of the way. I'll attend to you later.

"All right, now, you men," the commander repeated. "Are any of you qualified as divers?"

One of the men stepped forward.

"I'm not qualified, sir. But I've had a little experience with this kind of diving equipment."

The commander looked him up and down. His bulging muscles rippled across arms and shoulders that were bigger than the first diver's.

"If he couldn't make it, you can't," the commander snapped. "How about you other men?"

Silently, the men shook their heads.

Mike spoke up again.

"Sir, I tell you I can get in to those men. Just let me try, sir."

"The boy's right," Mr. Young agreed. "He could get those shoulders through where a full-grown man his height couldn't."

"Not a chance!" the commander shook his head sternly. "We'll put back to the base and get another diver."

"But, sir," Mike persisted. "You said yourself those men can't hold out very long. You'd never get back here in time."

"Son," the commander said, still shaking his head. "How old are you?"

"Fourteen, sir."

"I admire your courage, son. But do you realize that if I took a chance and authorized a deal like

[*129*]

this and anything went wrong, I'd be lucky to wind up as an apprentice seaman?"

"And if you don't," Mr. Young said quietly, "those men in there will be lucky not to wind up as fish food."

"You're right, of course, Young." The commander shrugged his shoulders. "I don't feel right about letting this boy take such a risk. But I can't abandon those men. What's your name, son?"

"Mike, sir. Mike Morrison."

"All right, Mike. You say you've used these diving lungs before?"

"To tell you the truth, sir," Mike replied, "not very much. But I've done a lot of skin-fishing with a mask and flippers, and I've tried a dive or two with a lung pretty much like this one. I can handle it, sir."

"Now listen carefully, Mike," the commander continued. "Your life as well as the lives of those men in there is going to depend on your avoiding mistakes. Did you follow closely when Mr. Young briefed the diver on the *Arapahoe's* construction?"

"Yes, sir. And besides, I know these ships pretty well. I've been all through them quite often."

The commander's eyebrows went up.

"Yes?" he asked quizzically. "And just how did you arrange that?"

"Well, sir, you see, my father is Captain Morrison, and I—"

"Oh, great!" the commander groaned. "The captain will kill me before he busts me, when he finds out about this!"

Then he grinned broadly. "Well, I must say," he added, "you're your old man's son."

Quickly he snapped back to business.

"All right. Let's go over this plan once more to fix it firmly in your mind."

Five minutes later, Mike was stripped down to his shorts and ready to go. The tank on his back felt as though it weighed a ton, but he knew that he wouldn't notice its weight once he was in the water. He took a few deep breaths of oxygen and found that he could breathe easily.

Then, with the coil of rope over his shoulder and a waterproof flashlight fastened by a cord to his belt, he started down the ladder that led over the launch's side.

Commander Mason patted him on the back.

"Take care of yourself, Mike," he said.

Mike slid off the ladder and down into the dark, oily water.

CHAPTER THIRTEEN

Inside the Sunken Ship

WHEN the water closed over his head, Mike's first feeling was one of terror. Below him, everything was pitch black, and the underside of the *Arapahoe* curved downward into nothingness.

He clenched his teeth inside the mask and started down, propelling himself along by frog-kicking with the rubber fins on his feet. He snapped on the flashlight and held it in front of him. Its beam was feeble as it stabbed into the blackness, but it gave enough light for him to make out the details of the ship's hull as he swam alongside it.

His confidence came back with a rush. This wasn't too bad! Not much different from spearing fish off the beaches of Kaneohe Bay! Just darker, that was about all!

Mike found the porthole that Mr. Young had told him to look for. It was hanging open. No wonder the big diver couldn't make it! Mike had the awful feeling that he wouldn't get through it either, with this bulky equipment strapped to him.

He turned over on his back, grasped the edge of the opening above him, and tried to wriggle himself inside. The tank scraped along the edge of the steel, and Mike rubbed his chest raw. But it was no use. The porthole was too small, and Mike with the air tank on his back was too big!

Then he remembered that the diver had muttered something about unstrapping the tank and trying to drag it after him. That was going to be risky business, but it looked like the only way.

Carefully, he unfastened the straps that went between his legs. The upper part of the tank was secured to his shoulders, but the lower part now hung free.

Slowly, very slowly, so as not to foul his air-line, Mike went through the porthole feet first. He ducked his head down, wormed his shoulders through and pulled the tank in after him. Hanging onto the edge of the porthole with one hand, he re-fastened the straps between his legs.

Whew! That had been too close for comfort!

He clung to the porthole for another minute until his breathing returned to normal, and then he took his bearings.

His flashlight didn't help much. Its shaft of light dissolved into the darkness a few feet in front of his face. Well, he'd have to navigate by dead reckoning!

He went over Mr. Young's chart in his mind and decided on his direction. He unwound a third of the coil of rope from his shoulder and let it dangle in the water. Taking a deep breath of oxygen, he shoved off into the black void, trailing the rope behind.

Mike knew that this particular compartment couldn't be more than thirty feet from wall to wall. But the seconds seemed like hours as he swam across it in the dark. Just as the terrifying thought crossed his mind that he had become lost and was probably wandering up some blind alley he would never get out of, his light picked up the solid bulk of the opposite wall.

He grabbed at an object that protruded from it. Then he smiled under the mask, and if there had been any sun down in this watery hole his eyes would have sparkled. He was clutching one of the dogs of the watertight door!

His flashlight didn't help much

Boy, he thought, that was what you called hitting it on the nose! This was easy!

He strained at the heavy dogs. Underwater, he seemed to have no strength at all. To make it even more difficult, there was nothing to stand on to get leverage. But slowly, as he pulled at the big iron bars, they swung around on their pivots and Mike pushed the door open.

Now he was overflowing with confidence. He unwound more line, again took his bearings, and once more shoved off with his flippered feet. In seconds he reached the farther wall.

But this time he wasn't so lucky. There was no watertight door in the weak beam of his light.

Again Mike went over the chart in his mind. The door should be not too far off to his right. He swam slowly along the wall, playing his flashlight as he went. Farther and farther he slid along the smooth, metal wall, but still no door. At last he came to a corner of the room, where the wall ended.

For an instant Mike panicked. Had he got himself completely turned around in his swim across the compartment? Was he so thoroughly lost down here in the dark that he'd never even be able to find the door through which he had entered? His first frantic impulse was to strike out wildly and look for it before it was too late.

Then he remembered the line that trailed behind him. What a dope! He could always follow it back and start over!

With his nerve in hand again, Mike began to think clearly once more. And suddenly Mr. Young's warning flashed into his head: *"Don't forget, everything will be upside down."*

Of course! That was it! The floor was the ceil-

ing, and the ceiling was the floor! And that made right left and left right! He'd simply turned the wrong way!

Mike started back along the wall the way he had come, and in less than a minute he was tugging and hauling on the heavy dogs that secured the second door.

When he pushed it open and slid through, he could make out in the light of his torch the dim outlines of the bodies of six men dangling in the

water just above him. He swam upward toward them, and his head broke out into the air pocket.

Out of the water, his flash threw a clear, strong beam of light that illuminated the pitch blackness.

Never in his life had he seen such expressions on any human faces. When he popped out of the water without warning and into their midst, the men stared goggle-eyed, terrified, as a man might if a grotesque, green-skinned, three-eyed, nine-legged Martian strolled into his living room.

The men were hanging onto pipes that ran along the wall. In spite of the fact that they had been submerged in water up to their necks for some hours, their faces were covered with a greasy coating of thick, oily sweat.

They continued to stare, unbelieving. Then the spell was broken, and they began to laugh and yell and pound Mike on the back.

Mike unfastened his mask and took it off. The stale air in the pocket struck him like a slap in the face. It was hot and damp and foul-smelling, and when he drew it into his lungs it was almost as though he was getting no oxygen from it at all. Mr. Young had been right. These men couldn't have lasted much longer.

Mike grinned. "Hi!" he said. "Don't you guys

know you oughtn't to hang around a stuffy place like this? You ought to get out in the fresh air."

The men grinned as they panted for breath.

Mike held the mask out to the nearest man.

"Here," he said, "take a whiff of this."

The sailor reached for the mask almost frantically.

"Careful!" Mike warned. "That's a short hose. Don't pull it loose!"

The man held the mask to his face and breathed in great lungfuls of the life-giving oxygen. After a minute, Mike tapped him on the shoulder.

"Give the other fellows a turn, and we'll pass it around again before we shove off."

As the fresh oxygen flowed into their starved bloodstreams, it gave the men new energy, new life. Now, Mike decided, was the time to make their try.

"Say," one of the sailors said, "aren't you awful young to be a Navy diver?"

"Well, I'm not exactly in the Navy yet," Mike told him. "But I was the only one who could squeeze in here with this rig."

He looked around at the men. Fortunately none of them looked too big to get out the porthole. One of them, maybe. But . . .

"God bless you for trying, kid," the sailor said. "I'm going to dance at your wedding. And anytime you ever lack for spending money, you just come around to the Navy Yard and ask for Charlie Lake."

"I just might take you up on that, Charlie," Mike said, smiling.

"Anytime, kid. Anytime at all."

"Okay," Mike said. "Now let's get out of here."

He pulled in the line until most of the slack was taken up and one of the men tied it around a pipe.

Mike explained the plan of escape.

"It's a long underwater swim out there," he warned. "You may have to hold your breath for more than a minute. But it's your only chance."

The men nodded silently.

"I think we'd better go one at a time," Mike said. "There might be a traffic jam if everybody tried it at once. I'll swim ahead of each man with my light to guide him along the line faster."

"Good deal," Charlie Lake said. "I'll be anchor man. Lindquist, you go first."

"All right, Lindquist," Mike said. "Wrap your arm around the line loosely so you can slide along it like a trolley. That way you won't get lost. Never mind trying to paddle with your hands. Just kick hard with your feet. You make better time that way under water."

"Got you, skipper," Lindquist said. "I'm ready any time you are."

Skipper! That was what Jeff had called him back on the *Mister Mike*. That seemed a long time ago!

"Let me get down through the first door with the light," Mike said. "Then you come on."

Mike put the mask over his face, and Charlie Lake helped him adjust it securely. He looked at Lindquist. The sailor nodded. Mike slid down into the water.

He waited a few yards from the opposite side of the opening until he saw Lindquist come through. Then, with his right arm hooked around the line, he swam as hard as he could for the second door. When he went through it he stopped and looked around. Lindquist was right behind him, kicking furiously.

Mike took off for the porthole that led to the safety of the harbor above them and, when he reached it, held his light so Lindquist could see it.

Lindquist slid through like a greased eel. Mike followed the line back to the air pocket.

One by one, Mike guided the trapped sailors along the line to the escape hole. And, one by one, they slithered through it to safety.

Charlie Lake was the last man. Mike looked a little dubious as Charlie prepared to leave the air pocket. Lake was the biggest of the group. But maybe he could get through. At least he had to try. It was his only chance.

Mike gave Charlie one final whiff of oxygen from his mask. Then he ducked under the water and out through the first door. Charlie followed, holding his breath, swimming furiously.

They made it to the porthole. Charlie squirmed and struggled to get his shoulders through. They were too big. Without a second's hesitation, Lake swam back along the line to the temporary safety of the air pocket. Mike followed at his heels.

When Mike's head broke the surface of the water in the pocket, Lake was hanging onto a pipe, as he had been when Mike first saw him, hungrily gulping the thin, fetid air into his lungs. Mike took off his mask and handed it to the nearly suffocated sailor. Charlie inhaled deeply, and soon his breathing had returned to normal.

"Sorry, kid," Charlie Lake said at last. "I'm afraid I'm just too big to make it. You go on and get out. I'll hang on here till the whistle blows."

"Nuts!" Mike said. "We've got a slogan in the Navy. Don't give up the ship. We'll just have to figure this out."

"You start figuring, kid," Charlie said. "I'm with you all the way."

"Look," Mike said. "When you get to that port-hole, stick one arm straight out and tuck your head under it, like this. Hunch up your shoulder so that it covers your head. Hunch your other shoulder and arm down in a straight line with your body. Then go out arm and head first. If that doesn't work on the first try, hustle on back here and we'll try to think of something else."

"Okay, skipper," Charlie said. "Give me one more drag on that oxygen, and then we'll get going."

They made it to the escape hole again. This time, Charlie started through as Mike had suggested. It was a tight squeeze. Mike got behind him and pushed. Then, like a cork popping out the neck of a bottle, Charlie was on the outside and heading for the surface and safety.

Mike unstrapped the air tank from his back, and went out the same way he had come in.

Safely outside the ship, he headed for the surface. His head broke water at the launch's ladder.

A dozen eager hands hauled him on deck and stripped off his diving gear.

Then such a yell went up as Mike had never heard. Everybody wanted to pound him on the back at once. The men from the sunken *Arapahoe* couldn't seem to keep their hands off him.

Lindquist, the first sailor who had escaped, threw his arms around Mike's neck.

"Look, kid," he shouted gleefully, "pay no mind to that Charlie Lake. You ever want any spending money, you come to me."

"Nuts!" another of the men yelled. "If this kid ever needs anything, he comes to old Hank Kane!"

"You ever join the Navy, kid," a third man put in, "I'll be proud to serve under you any time!"

The motor of the launch roared into life, and she headed back toward the Navy Yard.

"All right, men," Commander Mason shouted over the yelling. "Give the boy a chance to get his breath. He's earned it."

He stuck out his hand.

"Son," he said, "the Navy owes you a debt it can never repay. And so do I."

He shook Mike's hand in a firm, warm grip.

"Doggone it!" He grinned. "I said you were your old man's son!"

CHAPTER FOURTEEN

Home Again

THE sun was setting over the high ridges of the Waianae Mountains to the west and it was growing dark as Mike walked wearily up Makalapa Drive toward his house on the heights.

He was bone tired. His head throbbed with a dull ache from the pounding of the bombs and the pressure of the water inside the sunken *Arapahoe*. The muscles of his arms and shoulders were sore, and he could feel the beginnings of charley-horse symptoms in the calves of his legs.

Even though he had taken a hot shower after his return to the Naval Base in Commander Mason's launch, his hair was still matted and greasy from the thick oil that had covered the waters of the harbor.

The lights were on in the Morrison living room as he crossed the front porch and opened the door.

His father and mother sat side by side on the sofa. Apparently, the captain had arrived only a few minutes before Mike, for his face was dirty and grime-streaked, and his uniform, so white and stiffly starched that morning, was wrinkled and smudged with smoke and grease. Its high, stiff collar was open at the throat.

"Well, son," he said as Mike entered the room, "we had ourselves quite a day."

Mike looked around.

"Where's Jeff?" he asked.

"Still out at the field," his father said. "They're working around the clock trying to get a few fighters and bombers ready to welcome the Japs when they come back."

"Do you still think they're coming back, Dad? Everybody figured they'd strike again this afternoon, but they didn't."

"I don't know, son," Captain Morrison said. "I honestly don't know. Every rule in the book says they should—and probably with a landing force this time to try and take the islands. Of course," he added thoughtfully, "every rule in the book said they shouldn't have attacked us in the first

[*148*]

house opened, and Mary Jane stepped out onto the dew-wet grass.

This time Mike wasn't sarcastic. He'd seen Mary Jane in action yesterday. She was a good soldier. She'd do to have on your side!

"Hi, there!" he called. "I'm glad you and Jeff got home all right."

"We had a dreadful time, Mike," Mary Jane said. "All those planes started shooting at us, and then we went up to Wheeler, and when we got there the field was bombed out and——"

"Look," Mike interrupted. "The Army is fortifying the beaches from Waikiki clear around Koko Head and all up the tip of the island. I thought I'd ride out there and see the fun. Why don't you get your bike and come along? You can tell me all about it on the way."

"Wait a minute," Mary Jane said, "while I leave a note for Mama."

In a few minutes they were coasting side by side down Makalapa Drive. They wheeled past the Navy Yard, where crews of workmen were busy with cranes and bulldozers clearing away yesterday's wreckage; into the long, straight stretch of Kamahamaha Highway; across the bridges and down Dillingham Boulevard into Honolulu itself.

The streets of the city were just starting to come to Monday morning life. Nowhere, as they rode through the almost deserted streets, could they see any signs of damage from the raid. The quiet, sleepy city seemed to be separated by a million miles from the almost complete devastation of the Naval Base and Hickam Field, only a few miles away.

One thing about the Japs, Mike thought, they've got good shooting eyes!

They pedaled through the business section of Honolulu, out the quiet residential streets of Kaimuki and past the golf course of the Waialae Country Club. Here they encountered the first Army patrols and the first sign of barb-wire.

A tough Army private, his rifle slung under his right arm, stopped them.

"Where do you kids think you're going?" he demanded.

"Please, sir," Mike said, thinking fast, "we're just trying to get home."

"And where's home?"

"Lanikai Beach, sir," Mike said, enjoying the story that he was making up as he went along. "We were in the city yesterday visiting our cousins up on St. Louis Heights when the bombs started falling on the harbor. Aunt Hester made us stay there all night, but if we don't get home soon, Mother will be worried and—"

"All right. All right," the soldier said. "Go on home. But don't get off the main road or you may get into trouble."

As they pedaled off, Mary Jane looked at Mike and laughed.

"I'll bet you don't know Aunt Hester's last name," she giggled.

"Look," Mike said, "there's a war on. The less you tell people the better."

Their story about Aunt Hester, repeated each time they came to an Army barracade, got them past the beaches of Maunalua Bay, across the causeway to Koko Head, and around the eastern tip of the island.

Everywhere they went, the Army was working furiously, stringing barb-wire, putting up tents, setting up gun emplacements, getting ready for the Jap invasion. They slipped by convoys of Army trucks loaded with food, ammunition, supplies, and yelling, cheering soldiers; and equally long lines of empties returning to Schofield and Shafter for more.

At one point, a squad of soldiers had bottles of Coke cooling in a large, wooden bucket of ice water. The sergeant in charge, a big, jolly, loud-laughing fat man, insisted that Mike and Mary Jane stop long enough to have one.

By now the sun had become very hot, and the sergeant didn't have to insist twice.

THE FIRST JAP PRISONER

It was ten o'clock by Mike's watch when they slid down the mountainside to the beach at Kane-ohe. They leaned their bikes against a rough outcropping of coral rock.

"I've got on swimming trunks under my shorts," Mike said.

"And I've got a bathing suit tied to my bike," said Mary Jane.

"Then what are we waiting for?" Mike asked. "Get over behind that rock and put it on, and we'll cool off."

The tangy sea water was wonderfully brisk and refreshing after their long bike ride, and Mike and Mary Jane ran and splashed and dived in the surf and swam out beyond the white line of breakers and in to the sand again.

"Come on," Mike said, as they lay toasting themselves in the sun. "Let's take a walk up the beach."

Strolling slowly along in the warm sand, enjoying the sound of the surf and the pleasant smell of the sea, they rounded a rocky point. A hundred yards ahead of them, a group of soldiers were crowded around an object that had been washed up by the tide.

It was shaped like a fat, stubby cigar. The stern

end was smashed, exposing a tangle of pipes and wiring and the remains of a twisted propeller. A short conning tower, battered and bent, thrust itself up near the bow.

The strange craft was not more than forty feet long and could have easily fitted into the Morrisons' back yard.

Mary Jane and Mike broke into a run.

When Mike tried to shoulder his way through the ring of soldiers, a sentry roughly shoved him back.

"Beat it, you kids!" he ordered. "What are you doing here anyway? Get lost!"

Mike backed away and climbed up on the top of a coral rock. From here he had a good view of the badly battered midget submarine.

"What is it, Mike?" Mary Jane asked anxiously.

"It's a sub," Mike said. "A Japanese submarine."

"A sub?" Mary Jane said incredulously. "It can't be! It's too *little!*"

"That's a midget sub," Mike told her. "I've heard Dad talk about them. They have a crew of one or two men and they're carried into action piggyback on the big submarines. Boy! I'll bet the harbor was crawling with them yesterday!"

"But where are the men who were in her?" Mary Jane asked. "She looks all smashed up."

"That's probably what happened to the men," Mike said. "She looks as if she took a hard hit from something, maybe a depth charge from a destroyer. The crew may still be inside her, or maybe they were blown out by the explosion that wrecked her. Or it could be," he said, "that they abandoned ship."

Mary Jane shivered. "I don't care where they are," she said. "Let's get out of here."

They slipped their shorts on over their wet bathing suits, mounted their bikes, and started back the way they had come.

Past Bellows Air Field, which had been as thoroughly bombed out as Wheeler and Hickam, and was littered with the mangled shapes of what had been fighter planes, the road dropped down almost to the water's edge.

They stopped for a moment to rest and look out over the long lines of white-capped breakers that rolled in from far out in the blue sea like orderly rows of marching soldiers and tumbled on top of each other on the sandy beach.

"Like to take one more swim before we head back for the city?" Mary Jane asked.

"What I'd like more than anything else," Mike

replied, "is something to eat. I just remembered that I didn't have breakfast this morning and I'm starving."

Mary Jane unhooked the straps of the big leather bag that hung behind the saddle of her bike.

"Why didn't you say so?" she said. "I fixed a couple of sandwiches before I left. Here. Will cream cheese do?"

They leaned on their bikes while they munched their food and gazed idly over the water.

Looking up the deserted beach, Mike's eye caught a fleeting glimpse of a dark object that lay on the sand. The foremost edge of the incoming breakers washed up to it, lapped around it, and then receded.

"Look up there," he said, pointing. "What's that?"

Mary Jane shaded her eyes and peered hard.

"Why, Mike," she exclaimed, "I believe I saw it move!"

"By golly," he said, "I think you're right. It might be a baby porpoise or something that got washed in by the surf and can't get back into the water. At least it's too small to be another sub. Come on, let's go and see."

They raced up the beach.

"Mike!" Mary Jane stopped suddenly and clutched his arm. "Look, Mike! It's a body!"

They approached it cautiously.

The man lay sprawled on his back. He was short and dark-skinned, and his jet-black hair was cropped close to his head. He was barefooted and bare-waisted, and wore only a faded pair of khaki pants.

Mary Jane averted her eyes, but she couldn't help stealing an occasional curious glance.

"Poor, poor man," she said. "He was probably out in his fishing boat when the bombing started."

Mike leaned over and took a closer look. Then he straightened up in alarm.

"This is no native, Mary Jane! This is a Jap!" he gasped.

The Japanese groaned and opened his eyes.

"This is no native, Mary Jane! This is a Jap!"

Mary Jane screamed. "He's alive! Run, Mike! Run!"

Mike looked around and picked up a piece of coral rock slightly larger than a baseball.

"Look, Mary Jane," he said coolly, "this guy is in no shape to hurt anybody. Hop on your bike and go back up the road to Bellows Field for help. If he comes to enough to make trouble," Mike hefted the piece of coral in his hand, "I can handle him. But," he added hastily, "hurry!"

Mary Jane flew back to her bike and climbed on. As she turned into the road, a soldier with a big automatic pistol slung in a holster at his hip came sauntering down the road. He was a native Hawaiian, and wore the khaki uniform of the Hawaiian National Guard.

"What's up, missy?" he asked cheerfully.

As Mary Jane blurted out her story, his eyes went wide and his mouth fell open. He started off down the beach at a gallop, unfastening the flap of his holster as he ran. Mary Jane pounded at his heels.

The Japanese was sitting up, his elbows on his knees and his head in his hands. He was muttering in a harsh, guttural tongue that Mike had never heard before.

[*165*]

He looked up into the muzzle of the soldier's pistol and tried to stand.

Mike threw away his stone and helped the Jap to his feet. He stood staggering, turning his head slowly and looking around in a daze.

The big Hawaiian guardsman grinned, his white teeth flashing in his chocolate face.

"Kids," he said, "it looks like you've just captured the first Jap prisoner of the war!"

His smile widened with satisfaction.

"And I," he added, "am taking him in. I'll get a sergeant's stripes for this."

CHAPTER SIXTEEN

Purple Heart and Navy Cross

MIKE struggled with the studs of his new dress shirt. His new white linen dinner jacket, the first he had ever owned, hung over the back of a chair.

Jeff looked in the open door and laughed at his brother's clumsiness. He wore a shiny new uniform, and his Air Corps wings glistened silver over his left breast pocket.

"Here," he offered, "let me give you a hand with that."

"What's all this about getting dressed up for dinner at the club?" Mike demanded. "Usually, I'm not even allowed to go there at all."

"This is a special mission, kid," Jeff said. "Now take it easy and relax. Besides, it's my last night at home."

"Here," Jeff offered, *"let me give you a
hand with that."*

Mike looked serious. "Where do you think they'll send you, Jeff?"

"Your guess is as good as mine. My orders say report Stateside for reassignment. That's all I know. Now that we're at war with Germany too, it may be England. But I hope it's back to the Pacific. I want another crack at the Japs. They owe me about ten more *Zeros.*"

A month had gone swiftly by since the surprise attack of December 7th. Repairs to the Navy Yard installations had been made miraculously fast. Crews of experts, flown out from San Francisco, were refitting the ships damaged in the battle. Work was already under way to refloat the *West Virginia,* the *Oklahoma,* and the other brave ships that lay sunken on the bottom of the harbor, and make them ready to fight again.

The airfields had been cleared, the runways and hangars repaired. Fresh squadrons of fighters and bombers were arriving every day to build the Air Corps up to wartime effectiveness.

"You know, Jeff," Mike said thoughtfully as he adjusted his black bow tie, "I've often wondered why the Japs didn't come back that day."

"So has everybody," Jeff replied. "We sure didn't have much to fight with after their bombers got through. But it's too late for them now. They'll never pull one like that again. And," he added, "I hope that goes for any future enemy."

He slapped his kid brother affectionately on the shoulder.

"Get a move on. The folks are waiting for us."

The dining room at the Officers' Club was gaily decorated with Hawaiian flowers. In a corner of the room, a native orchestra played soft island music. Seated around the great horseshoe of tables

were most of Hawaii's high-ranking Army and Navy officers.

Captain Morrison led his family to a place of honor at the speakers' table. Mary Jane was there with her father and mother. Mike found himself sitting next to her.

"This is quite a shindig," he whispered.

Native waiters served the food—big, sizzling steaks with all the trimmings, topped off by a dessert of a whole pineapple, standing upright in a mound of shaved ice and hollowed out so that the pieces of fruit swam in their own sweet juices.

Then the toastmaster, a high-ranking admiral, got to his feet and rapped on his glass with a spoon for attention.

"Ladies and gentlemen," he began, "we are here tonight to honor the brave men and women of our armed forces who fought so gallantly against overwhelming odds to defend this outpost of the United States against a treacherous attack by an infamous enemy. It is not possible to do individual honor to them all. Every one of them did honor to the uniform he wore, and, in the heat of battle, many brave deeds went unnoticed and unsung."

As the admiral's voice went on, Mike's mind slipped back to that unforgettable Sunday morning. He wondered what had happened to Pete and to the sailors they had pulled from the oily waters. And Lindquist, Charlie Lake, Hank Kane, and the other men who had been trapped in the *Arapahoe*. And that National Guard soldier. Had he got his sergeant's stripes for bringing in the Jap prisoner?

He saw Commander Mason's face smiling at him from across the room. The commander made a small gesture with his hand, halfway between a wave and a salute.

Then, as their names were called, the officers around the table stepped forward and received their citations and their medals.

"Captain Jeffrey Morrison, United States Army Air Corps!"

When his name was called, Jeff looked startled. Mike nudged him. "Go ahead. That's you."

"But—but he said *Captain*," Jeff stammered.

His father smiled. "Maybe he meant it," he said.

Jeff came back to the table with a big grin on his face. A Distinguished Flying Cross was pinned underneath his wings, and he carried the shiny, silver double-bars of a captain in his hand.

An Army nurse stepped forward. Her right arm was in a sling.

"Look, Mike," Mary Jane whispered. "That's the nurse I told you about. The one I helped at Wheeler Field."

The nurse returned to her seat wearing the Purple Heart.

The names went on and on. When his turn

came, Commander Mason was awarded the Navy Cross.

As the last name was called and the last decoration handed out, there was a resounding flood of applause. When it died down, the Army nurse arose to her feet.

"Sir," she addressed the admiral, "with your permission I would like to say a word."

The admiral nodded assent.

"I deeply appreciate this honor," the nurse went on, "but I would like to share it with someone who deserves it far more than I do. While my other nurses and I were lying wounded and helpless at Wheeler Field that morning, a little girl stepped in and did the job we couldn't do. I saw her save at least one man's life that would have surely been lost without her. Her name is Mary Jane Fisher."

She looked up the long table to where Mary Jane sat wide-eyed. "Janie," she said, "I wish you'd wear this Purple Heart for me."

The applause was deafening, and before it had quieted Commander Mason was standing up.

"Sir," he said. "I have a similar request to make. The man who really earned this Navy Cross does not wear a United States Navy uniform. In years, he is not a man at all. But in courage and self-sacrifice, he is one of the finest men I have ever known."

The big room was silent as the commander spoke.

"He volunteered for a mission alone into a sunken ship, a mission my men were physically unable to undertake. And singlehandedly he saved the lives of six men who otherwise would still be entombed under the waters of Pearl Harbor to-night.

"Michael Morrison," he said, "it would do me great honor if you would wear this Navy Cross for me."

Once more, the applause was loud and long. When it was over, the admiral picked up an envelope from the table in front of him.

"Thank you, Commander," he said. "It just so happens that I, too, have something to say to young Mr. Morrison. I want to read him a letter."

He opened the envelope and adjusted horn-rimmed glasses to his nose.

"This letter is addressed to Mr. Michael Morrison, care of the commanding officer, United States Naval Base, Pearl Harbor. It reads as follows:

" *'Dear Michael: Reports have been forwarded to my attention regarding the heroic acts you performed, above and beyond any normal call of duty, during and after the Japanese attack of December 7th. Specific reference has been made to your underwater rescue of six enlisted men of the United States Navy who were hopelessly trapped in the wreck of a sunken minecraft.'* "

The admiral paused, looked up, smiled in Mike's direction, and continued:

" *'It has further come to my attention that you will be seventeen years of age on December 7, 1944. On that day, under the powers vested in my office, I will be pleased to appoint you to the United States service academy of your choice, as a Midshipman in the Naval Academy at Annapolis, or a Cadet in the Military Academy at West Point.'*

"And that letter, Mike," the admiral said, "is signed by the President of the United States."

The dining room exploded into an uproar of shouting and hand-clapping. People crowded around Mike, slapping him on the back and shaking his hand. His mother hugged him, and his father draped a big arm around his shoulders.

Jeff punched him on the arm, grinning with pride and affection.

[*176*]

"All right, kid," he said. "I told you you'd have to make up your mind about that uniform. What's it going to be? Air Corps khaki or Navy blue?"

Mike felt Mary Jane slip her small hand into his. He gave it a gentle squeeze.

"Gosh, Army," he said, "don't rush me. The man says I've got three more years to decide."

WE WERE THERE BOOKS